MADMAN'S ISLAND

Ion Idriess

INTRODUCED BY ERNEST HUNTER

ETT IMPRINT
EXILE BAY

Published by ETT Imprint, Exile Bay in 2020

First published in Australia in 1933 by Angus & Robertson. Reprinted (three times), 1934 (twice), 1936, 1937, 1938, 1939, 1941, 1942 (twice), 1944, 1947, 1949, 1951 (twice), 1962, 1966, 1967, 1973, 1977

ISBN 978-1-925706-97-0 (pbk)
ISBN 978-1-925706-98-7 (ebk)

Designed by Hanna Gotlieb
Internal drawings by Percy Lindsay

INTRODUCTION

Ernest Hunter

Forty-five years after HM Bark *Endeavour* rounded the tip of York Cape and headed west leaving in its wake new names for almost all the coastal landmarks of Australia's north-eastern shore, HM Brig *Kangaroo* became the first vessel to traverse the entire inner reef. In doing so it entered the area that Cook had missed between Lizard Island, where he headed to the safety of the open sea to escape *the labyrinth* through Cook's Passage, and Cape Weymouth where Providential Channel offered him the opportunity to find the way west that he knew was there. Charles Jeffreys, the master of the *Kangaroo,* was about as different to James Cook as an officer in the Royal Navy could be. A liar, plagiarist, and smuggler of hard liquor and lost souls, he had disobeyed the orders of Governor Macquarie in taking that route to Ceylon – just one of the reasons Macquarie wanted him court-martialled. True to form, with a concocted newspaper account of the journey through the reef, he eventually avoided court-martial and it may have helped that the first islands he encountered when he guided the *Kangaroo* into the uncharted sea north of Cook's Passage he named after Viscount Howick – who went on to become Prime Minister.

Just over a century later, three men who had recently returned from the First World War met in the bar of the West Coast Hotel in Cooktown – a town that was already in decline from the heady days of the Palmer River gold rush four decades before. All three carried the War with them in wounds of flesh and spirit and within a dozen years two were laid to rest in Cooktown cemetery – Dick Welsh and George Tritton. The third man, Ion Idriess, went on to become Australia's most popular author, mining recollections of his life in the bush for another four decades, alloying personal experience with extensive research to create vibrant cameos of pioneer life at the edge of the new nation. The circumstances, characters and attitudes were, however, already part of a frontier past; as much as Idriess was an indefatigable booster of outback development and the boundless opportunities of Australia's northern future, he was a man of his times – and times change.

In 1920, though, as the three ex-diggers talked across the bar at the West Coast, swapping stories of the War and goings-on in Cooktown and along the coast, the pioneer vision would have still been fresh and sustained by hope and dreams. All that was needed was a little luck – which might come from the Chinese gambling den across the way, or at the races, or a tip on a 'sure thing', be it trepang, trochus, timber or the treasures of the earth. So that day Idriess signed up for a sure thing with George Tritton – or perhaps not such a sure thing; Dick Welsh, Idriess's best mate, chose not to go. Even so, a few days later Jack (Idriess's frontier name) and George set sail for Howick Island. Before the end of the decade Idriess had renamed both the Island and his companion – he wrote that he had gone to Madman's Island with his mate, Charlie.

Idriess was already a writer, having contributed articles to *The Bulletin* as *The Gouger,* but his first book, released in 1927, was *Madman's Island.* Originally written as non-fiction, his publisher had advised that it be revised with changes to plot and characters to increase appeal, but that was not enough – it flopped. A decade later, after success with an account of service with the 5th Light Horse in Gallipoli and Palestine (*The Desert Column*), it was released close to it's original form as a factual account of his three months on Howick, only the real name of his companion undisclosed. This one sold, as did others – Ion Idriess was on a roll.

Two centuries have passed since Charles Jeffries named Howick Island and a century since Jack Idriess returned from the War to Cooktown from which he and George set out for what he would later call Madman's Island a year later. As what happened was the basis for his first book – the story that follows – it's an opportune time for a reconsideration of Ion Idriess who, despite selling some three million copies of more than fifty books, is no longer popular and seldom discussed by readers or critics.

At least not by literary critics; by contrast his work is increasingly challenged as representing the attitudes and prejudices typical of the first half of the twentieth century in Australia – particularly in relation to Indigenous Australians. That is, in fact, a fair observation and his description of Aboriginal and Torres Strait Islander Australians reflected what were conventional perceptions, be they of savagery or vulnerability. But in particular ways he was ahead of his time. His descriptions of Torres Strait Islanders, as warriors and workers, draws on the research of the 1897 Cambridge Expedition to the Torres Strait, and extensive discussions with local informants including travel to the outer islands with missionary-ethnographer W.H. MacFarlane. What he presented to his readers, wrapped around conventional plot devices, is a complex ethnographic portrayal of late 19th century Islander society on the cusp of radical transformation after the discovery of pearl-shell on Warrior Reef.

Idriess's descriptions of Aboriginal people are more complex and contentious, but he also stands as the first widely-read Australian author to write of Aboriginal resistance to the appropriation of their country, and of Aboriginal individuals as warriors and heroes – albeit tragic heroes. In *Nemarluk*, *The Red Chief*, and *Outlaws of the Leopolds* Idriess does not shy away from the righteousness and futility of resistance, even though he would not have questioned the imperial vision that, by then, had transmuted into popular understandings of 'progress'. While he gave colour to the tragedy he did not question it. Many of those sentiments are still with us, woven into our history and hidden in the fabric of social and political life. By taking us back to the raw encounters of our frontier heritage which were still ongoing in the first decades after Federation, reading Idriess challenges us to confront the conflict that he described but did not resolve, the afterglow of which remains with us a century later.

Madman's Island; Idriess as character and author – fact or fiction. Fifty books later the seam he struck after returning from the War was mined out. There was nothing left that could be said about frontier life as Idriess saw and said it. It required and still needs to be understood from other perspectives. But Ion Idriess – as Jack Idriess along the Bloomfield, in the Tablelands back of Cairns, and along the coast of north Queensland – gives us a participant's view. It's a voice we should attend to – it's our voice from a fading past.

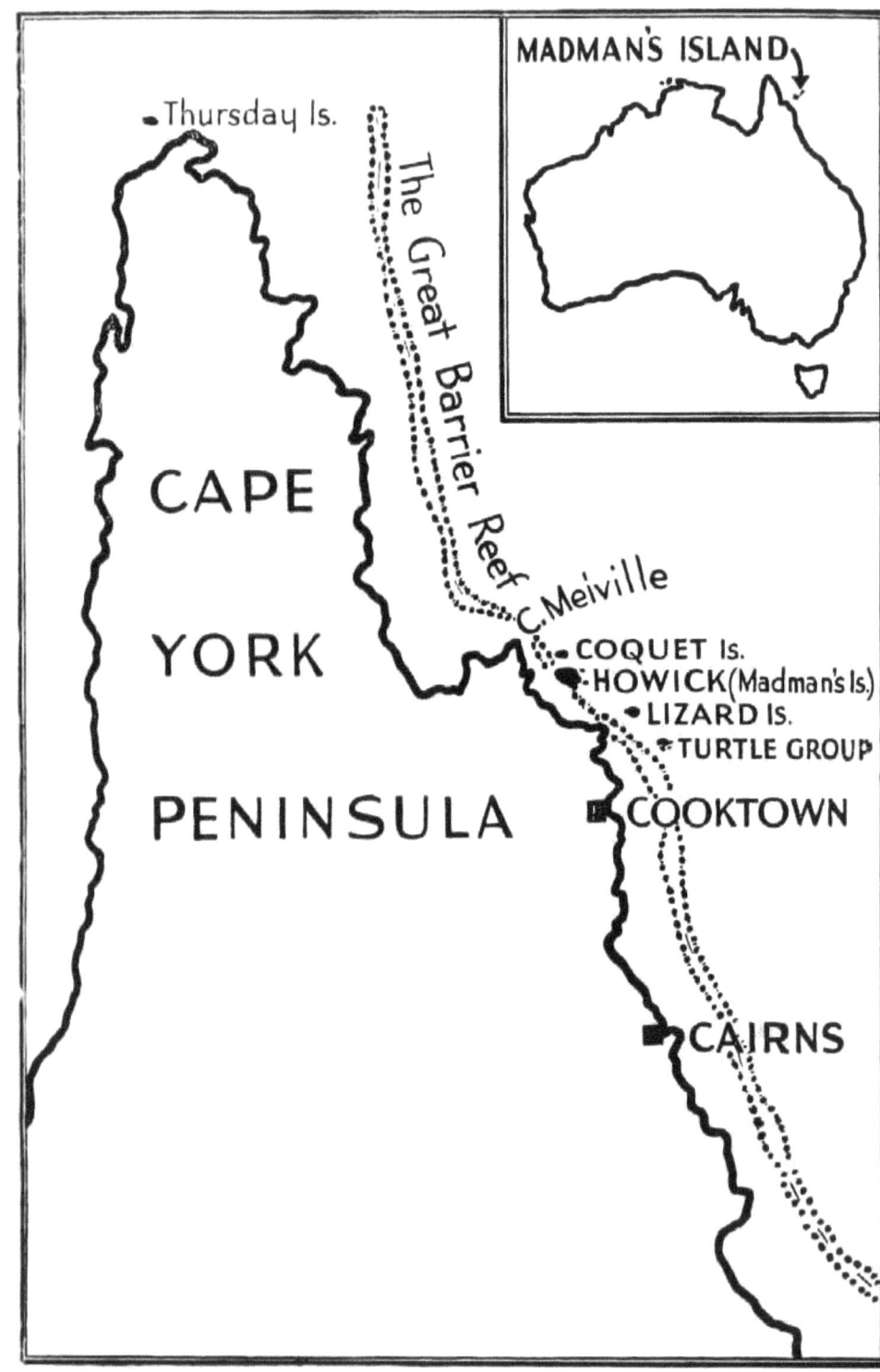

CONTENTS

1

The Island

We gazed at the island, its two tiny hills rising abruptly from the sea. It looked interesting, but unfriendly. There was no beauty of palm or glen, no sylvan scene awaiting us here. We could now see the grass tops rippling under the breeze, the sombre grey of boulders.

"A forlorn looking place," growled Charlie.

"It is!" agreed the skipper.

"Why the pleased gloom?" I remonstrated. "We're not going to live there for ever."

"I would not live there for ten minutes!" shrugged the skipper.

The cutter heeled over, bowing and dipping to the slap of playful waves. The aboriginal crew laughed uproariously at some joke at the white men's expense. Presently we saw the branches of mangroves that fringed the smaller hill. Fronting both hills was a collar of foam where lazy waves broke in over a reef. Between the hills but beyond them peeped a black mass that was a forest of trees. The skipper pointed towards the reef:

"Old Tarquay's boat was wrecked just there. He and a blackboy swam ashore but the other boy was cut to pieces upon the coral. Why you two apparently sensible men insist on coming to this isolated hole, amazes me."

"Tarquay found tin there!" growled Charlie.

"He *says* he did. Well, it is your funeral, not mine."

But I felt happy. The bright blue sky, the lazily rolling sea, the gulls wheeling overhead, all combined in making life feel so wild and free. And here was a brand new island—our very own. I smiled at the glum cheerfulness of the skipper and winked at my mate's grim face as he frowned towards the island.

Charlie *was* on the sombre side. Little wonder. He had been drinking heavily in Cooktown, and his wild eyes, deeply lined face and grizzly black moustache made him appear positively savage. A week at sea in a tiny craft buffeted by wayward winds had not improved him. But there would be no drink on this tiny island. Dick and I had met Charlie for the first time when recently we returned to Cooktown from a long prospecting trip in the Bloomfield-Daintree mountains. Charlie had installed himself as "honary" barman in the West Coast Hotel. To Dick and me, he threw over the bar counter several small black stones.

"What do you think of those?" he growled.

"They're tin!" replied Dick as he examined the little black specimens.

"Picked up on the beach," explained Charlie, "at Howick Island by Tarquay the Malay. His cutter was wrecked there. A Jap pearler rescued him and landed him at Cooktown only a week ago."

"There might be a good show on that island then," said Dick.

"These specimens are rich."

"Looks like a rich reef where they came from," growled Charlie confidentially as he leaned over the bar. "How about prospecting the island?"

"Not on your life," laughed Dick. "The land and the old horses will do me. On an island I'd feel like a fish out of water."

So Charlie and I had agreed on a short trip to the island. A supply ketch, due soon to sail up the Cape York Peninsula coast with supplies for an inland mining field, would land us on the island with a month's provisions. The skipper would call back for us, weather permitting, and we could return to Cooktown. If we located payable mineral, he would take us back to the island, with fuller equipment and provisions.

Thus started my first experience of island prospecting, despite friendly warnings about Charlie. He had come down from the heart of the Musgrave Ranges up the Peninsula north of Cooktown to spend his little bar of gold. Up there, as a hatter, he had toiled alone, living like a "nigger" among the aboriginals. This well-meant information rather drew me towards him for I have always been interested in the aboriginals. Charlie must be a cool, level-headed chap with grit and initiative and a lot of the primitive in his make-up to have existed for years amongst the natives. Now, he was squatting against the mainmast, hatless, peering out over the bows from piercing eyes deep set under shaggy brows. Tall with the beginnings of a stoop, his gaunt frame suggested endurance. His bare, hairy chest and brown, muscled arms were not those of the weakling. Living like a native had done him no physical harm.

Mentally, he appeared as sane as myself. Those warnings of the men from the Far North were well meant but exaggerated. Charlie had been so seriously wounded in France that he was compelled to carry "a whole chemist's shop" about with him. After a long drinking bout he might forget to doctor himself up; when he did, he was liable to go off his head for a time. Rumour said he had been under official detention on occasion.

The skipper brought the ketch up into the wind and ordered: "Stand by the dinghy!" With idly flapping sails our craft lay just off the reef, gently rolling as the native crew jumped to the dinghy and dropped her overboard. Two leapt in while their comrades handed down the cases of provisions. Charlie rose with a grunt.

"I daren't go closer," pointed the skipper. "See there, down under the green, the coral wall is just waiting for a ship. Our luck is right in or we could not come so close. There is no anchorage here. Even with a moderate sea it is impossible to land, because of the reef."

"What odds!" said Charlie. "We're landing now."

The skipper shrugged as Charlie slung the swags down into the dinghy then climbed cautiously after them. A tinge of uneasiness followed me down among the cases beside Charlie; this island might hold grim possibilities if weather were to prevent a boat landing to take us away.

With a chatter and laugh to their comrades the boys pushed off.

"Good luck," waved the skipper.

"Don't leave us marooned here!" I called back.

"Never fear: back when you want me."

Skilfully handled by the two boys the dinghy rose with a wave and skimming over the reef was quickly in the calmer water of a miniature lagoon, and in a few minutes was being manoeuvred among the mangrove-trees to ground on the crushed coral of the tiniest beach in the world. We slung' the cases ashore and the boys, cheerfully receiving their sticks of tobacco, rowed back to the waiting ketch. The dinghy was smartly hauled aboard, the sails filled to the wind, foam kissed the bows as the vessel sheered away. Faintly came their hail of farewell.

2

Camp Mates

In the liveliest of spirits we commenced rigging a camp.

"I'll cut the tent poles," suggested Charlie as he unpacked the axe, "while you put the billy on. The well must be over there down by the mangrove edge. See! There is old Tarquay's track."

From a rude shelter of wreckage nearby, a track, just discernible in the grass, led apparently towards the back of the island. I followed expectantly this path worn by the feet of the Malay and his man Friday. It climbed a few yards to where the bases of the two tiny hills met. A hundred yards farther on appeared the edge of a dull green mangrove forest that stretched apparently two or three miles out to sea. Only mangroves; but a welcome sight, showing that the island was not so very small. Walking down along the grass-lined track I turned and gazed back at the two hills. They stood up like giant's thumbs hedged around .by an immensity of sea and sky. The call of a bird came pleasantly. The hill-sides were scarred by the tiniest of ravines, dark green with dwarf trees whose tops had been flattened by many winds.

Everywhere else the little hill slopes appeared green with grass except for the grey of granite boulders reflecting the sun. The hill to the right was really a grassy peak; the other was more nuggety, dotted with more boulders and a few more scrubby trees. The area of the island above tide-water would hardly cover ten acres; it was a puzzle why centuries of storms had not washed it away.

Again a bird trilled greeting away up there, and again it sounded comforting. Turning down the track again I walked across a patch of gently sloping ground formed by erosion from the Peak by wind and rain, where the wall of mangrove-frees began.

Rich loam, this small level patch, for the grass was profuse and green. Then the track led into the gloomy mangroves and the mud itself. Surely there could never be fresh water here! I peered doubtfully among the trees. A sudden fluttering, a chorus of excited chirpings as dripping birds flew up from a circular ring of stones. It was the well; a real mystery of nature, a spring of fresh water welling up from below the salt-water mud. To keep the water sweet, aborigines ages ago had roughly cemented a collar of stones around the spring. This held back the tidal water which at big tides must rise two feet deep around the little protecting wall.

But what if the salt tides by some means should break into that water while we were on the island!

Back at the camp, Charlie already had the tent rigged, sheltered from the sea winds by the mangroves that hedged the miniature beach. To the right, the Peak rose straight up. To the left, the Hill. Behind was a ridge (only a mound of earth) that connected the Peak and Hill. If the island had been an envelope and the tent a postage stamp Charlie could not have placed the camp in a more correct position. He had been very busy too. I laughed to the implied reproach of the fiercely burning fire.

"You've certainly got a move on!"

"Yes. We must rig our bunks before sundown," he growled. "Put the billy on and I'll open this tin of beef. Some of that long grass will be just the thing for a mattress. We might as well make ourselves comfortable."

We enjoyed that meal, sitting there with the water lapping the beach not twenty feet away. Charlie thoughtfully munched, his eyes on the wreckage caught in the roots of the mangroves.

"The *Sea Foam?*" I inquired.

"Yes—some of it. There's flotsam, though, along the beach and in among the rocks, that must have drifted in from hundreds of miles away. There's enough timber close handy to build a comfortable hut."

"We won't want it; we'll be gone in a month."

Charlie stared at an inquisitive crab that was watching us from the sea edge. By sundown we had the camp fixed snug. Charlie's bunk was neat and shipshape; mine was rigged any old how.

"Let's inspect our kingdom," I suggested. "It's not often two men can boast they own a whole island between them."

So we climbed the Peak, a grassy cone two hundred and eighty feet high. From the summit our kingdom lay spread out below. Westward, the setting sun stained miles of rolling sea a glittering pink. Dimly to south and west, like a tracery of clouds, were mountains forming an uninhabited portion of the mainland coast. South, several dark clouds on the water were really islands. North too, just distinguishable, were others. East, like a gigantic, rapidly blackening carpet, stretched from our feet the mangrove forest, its farther edge dimming in the sea.

Windings of dulling silver glimpsed through the tree tops were salt-water creeks. It promised some weird exploring, that mangrove forest. Then we realized with pleasant surprise that we owned a third "hill" one thousand yards east on the sea edge of the mangroves. A bare, rocky knoll about sixty feet high—we christened it straightaway the "Mound." Connecting it now to our two hills was exposed a portion of the reef like a broad roadway a thousand yards long. From the outgoing tide the water was now rushing out of the mangroves and over it, back into the sea.

At low tide it would be quite easy to walk along the reef and explore the Mound and also the adjoining coral shore and mangroves. Enthusiastically we pointed out to each other what a lot of country we really had to explore —when the tide was out.

Darkness fell quickly, bringing up to us the murmur of the sea. We stood a while in the cool evening, watching the stars peep out. Rather a lonely feeling grew upon us. The island was so small; there was such a very little of it above water; we were so far from anywhere and anybody. We returned down through the grass to the campfire twinkling between the two hills, and to its cheery crackling put the billy on again. Charlie started whistling.

Night closed softly around us. Charlie sat staring into the fire, sipping his final pannikin of tea. Wavelets lapped among the mangrove roots on the tiny beach. Beyond these frontal trees gleamed a baby lagoon, and from out beyond came the slumbrous murmur of lazy waves rolling on its encircling reef.

"The camp is well protected. I believe we could last out a cyclone here," I remarked, blowing smoke lazily up towards the sky.

"Yes," growled Charlie, "so long as a man did not stand up or move twenty feet away from this hollow. If he did, he'd be blown into the lagoon, or else back over the little bank and into the mangrove forest behind."

"Ever been in a cyclone up north?"

Charlie slowly filled his pipe. He lit it with a coal from the fire before answering; just lifted the live coal with his fingers as natives do.

"Yes. On the Rocky River diggings during the Cape Melville cyclone. The goldfield is right up in the mountains, in the jungle.

Nine men were pinned under trees that night."

"Must have been a nasty experience."

"It was. In the dead of night the wind flattened the jungle. That roar was worse than any gunfire I ever heard in France. There were no trenches in that jungle, and nowhere to run to. Only darkness and howling rain and falling trees. The swelling creeks were soon dammed by falling trees, then they spilled over, burst the dams, and sent the trees crashing into the gorges. Men lay flat all night clinging to lawyer-canes and couldn't see a thing, only hear roaring water and crashing trees. It was hell in the morning. The jungle was uprooted trees piled twelve feet high."

He talked for two hours. Of hard-time struggles in the wild places of the continent, of finds of tin and wolfram and gold, of lonely wanderings in the heart of the Musgraves, his whereabouts known only to the blacks.

"Have you ever found a rich gold show, Charlie?"

"No, worse luck. I've found some promising shows and knocked a living out of them, but never a fortune. I've always done better at wolfram."

"What was the best show you ever found?"

"Nothing to the one I never found. I thought I could buy up all the millionaires in the world. I yelled at the mountain, I reckon I went mad for a while. It was near a favourite camp of mine, away out in the Musgraves. No one but niggers anywhere handy. It was wild country, all mountains and ravines and gorges. And I found a mountain of rubies! I nearly went crazy. A big gorge ran on down past the mountain and from an old dry river-bed in it I washed a dish of dirt and it was half full of rubies! I wore the skin oil my fingers washing the rubble. When the finger-tips were red raw I had to knock off. Then I traced the rubies to the mountain. The whole mountain was full of them, like blood-red plums in a mountain of hard grey dough. I was richer than Sinbad the Sailor.

From every dish in the river where the sand was caught against the rock bars I could wash a shovelful of rubies. I washed a ton of those rich reddish stones, then hand-picked a sugar bag full of the best and largest. I couldn't transport any more. Besides, I was terribly scared lest someone find out. I daren't land in Cooktown with packhorse loads of rubies! Anyway, if the mountain was discovered it would flood the market; rubies would become as cheap as dirt.

"I packed those rubies deep down in an old swag and took them over-land to Cooktown, caught the steamer and quietly sailed for Brisbane. When I offered the first handful to a jeweller and he told me they were garnets 1 assaulted him. I offered them to other jewellers. At last they convinced me they were not conspiring to rob me. So I got drunker than any man has ever been drunk before. And that night from my window rained my rubies down all over Queen Street."

"Stiff luck, Charlie. That is the biggest disappointment I've ever heard of in mining. I've known men clean up several tons of iron sands imagining they'd found a new tin field, but I never heard of finding a mountain of rubies before."

"A mountain of garnets!" answered Charlie grimly. "The damned impostors just about broke my heart."

"Aren't they of any value at all?"

"Very little. Hardly worth transportation. There's only a small market for the very pick of them."

He yarned then of the aboriginals. His aboriginal lore was fascinating. He had lived among wild tribes. I had too. But he had lived longer and travelled farther. Whereas I had had two half-caste mates and we travelled with the tribe, he had lived alone among them.

He could live in the bush with or apart from the natives, finding his own food. Every man whose livelihood takes him far from civilization for twelve months at a time wishes he could do that, should it ever become a matter of dire necessity. His horses might break away; eat poison weed, or be speared; he might be lost; in any eventuality when he might suddenly be cut off from foodstuffs he could thus live. Charlie could. My half-caste mates and I had, but differently. After the tribe had eaten our provisions, they fed us, as the most natural thing in the world to do. I had walked with them for month after month, accompanying the bucks on the hunt, watching the women seeking vegetable foods and fruit.

Charlie had learnt to do these things for himself and, what is more, to locate and prepare and cook vegetable foods. Numbers of vegetable foods contain poisonous substances and the blacks are adepts at the sometimes intricate treatment necessary to rid these foods of their poisons. Few white men can live on native foods. Except in favoured localities, it is awful stuff. But to know how to do so in case of emergency may mean the difference between life and death to a bushman.

It was intensely interesting listening to this man who must have had a lot of the primitive in him. It was in his husky voice as he talked, in the fire-lit glow of his eyes as he told of native vendettas, of the animal scream of a buck awaking with a spear between his ribs. He spoke of a night when he had crawled into the darkness, to find in daylight his sleeping-place riddled with spears. He told of "good niggers," and "bad niggers" and of the iron rule of the old men over all the tribe. Of the sure death of the young lubra who runs away with a lover, of the jungle law of "an eye for an eye". Listening, I wondered how much of that law he had imbibed himself. He talked until the fire burned low. Then stared at the coals. He answered several questions, but grew almost morose as is natural in a man recovering from the drink.

Yawning, I enjoyed a final pipe, then, slipping off my trousers, rolled in under the blanket.

3

Fright

"Shake a leg!" growled Charlie.

Reluctantly I awoke to the crackling of the fire. The billy was already boiled, the bacon fried. Charlie was sitting down to breakfast. It was as yet only the steel grey of dawn.

I slung off the blanket and grabbing the towel yawned down to the beach. The lagoon water was cool and so motionless that the floating sperm of fishes was like still brown patchwork upon it. As I returned to the fire a bird called to its mate from behind the little Peak.

"Sounds homelike, almost like the bush," I smiled.

"You won't hear many birds here," answered Charlie, "and what there are, are lazy. I had the billy boiled before the earliest took his head from under his wing."

I grinned. "He and I are birds of a feather."

In lively anticipation we prospected the beach, though it seemed futile and ridiculous to expect that mineral could be here in a mixture of shells, broken corals and sand. But in some dishes we did get a few colours of tin. The beach was so tiny that we had thoroughly prospected it by midday. In the afternoon we sank a line of potholes to water level at the sea base of the Peak, among big granite rocks that had rolled down from above. In one dish we got half an ounce of alluvial tin which proved at least that there *was* some tin—somewhere. But the beach was a failure. We discussed it over the campfire that night.

"The old Malay must have magnified his tin," I declared disappointedly.

"Perhaps not," mused Charlie. "Remember, he is no miner. He found reef tin for certain because he brought back specimens with him. We may have misunderstood his pidgin English directions and not located the right spot."

"He said the beach between the two hills. There are only two hills on the island, and we have tried that beach."

"Well! There was tin in it."

"Yes, just a prospect. It must have been denuded from the Peak or the Hill, and the waves have washed it back up on to the beach. But the prospects are so small that they cannot have come from a payable deposit."

"We can't be sure yet. Even in such a tiny area as this there may be a rich lode buried somewhere. We've got plenty of time to look around, anyway." He stirred the fire which responded cheerfully, lighting up his unsmiling face, his direct, thoughtful eyes. He was sparing with the wood though there was abundance of it as drift on the beach just a few yards away.

"Have you ever known the natives light a big fire?" I asked.

"No. Except at special corroborees or when firing the country in a game battle. Never otherwise, lest the fire betray them to enemies."

"Did a native ever attempt your life?"

"Yes—once!"

"What happened to him?"

Charlie stared into the fire, puffing at his pipe. ... A murmuring of waves came from the reef.

I stretched out on the blankets and gazed up at the velvet sky with its lure of twinkling stars. I was disappointed; the old Malay had been so positive of the rich tin to be found on the beach. Of course, any black-ish-looking stone might have deceived him as tin, especially as he really had found several specimens of the real mineral. I wondered what Dick was doing in distant Cooktown. What paddocks had he turned the old horses out in to spell? Would he go roaming away with some temporary mate before I returned?

What a difference there was in men! If Dick had been here we should have taken this island episode as a lark. But with Charlie it was going to be very different. We were temporary mates, but were worlds apart. Even now, I was beginning to think before I spoke. With Dick here I'd have said anything at any old time, just for the sake of a laugh.

Next morning, Charlie prepared to make a damper. He had a big fire blazing to provide the coals; the camp oven was being warmed while he cooked breakfast. I did the washing up. It was simple enough; I just put the plates and pannikins in the prospecting dish and poured a billy of hot water on them, then tipped them out on the grass to dry. To own a drying cloth would have meant that we should have had to keep on washing it.

Charlie mixed up his dough in a workmanlike fashion; flopped it in the camp oven; covered it with just the right amount of coals; then stepped to the beach to wash the flour from his hands. I was glad to see him tackle the damper; if there is any one thing I hate in bush life it is making a damper. Most men dislike making dampers and detest the dreary drudgery of washing clothes.

Permitted by the low tide, and our domestic arrangements for the day completed, we set out to explore, carrying our prospecting tools. A glorious day; we felt like walking miles instead of a miserable few hundred yards. As we passed the well by the mangrove edge little birds fluttered up with a cheeky greeting.

We stepped off the island on to the broad, grey-white road of the coral reef; the sea lazily walloped one side of it, the other was hedged in by the dense green wall of the mangrove forest. About a thousand yards ahead was the Mound, its domed top visible above the mangrove branches. I walked with boots on for coral is often sharp and some species of needle point are poisonous. But Charlie walked on bare feet, the soles tough as leather from years of bush walking without boots.

"Take care you don't get a poisoned leg from a coral splinter," I warned.

"We must get used to coral splinters," he growled.

I laughed. "No need. We probably won't be here more than a month at most."

"You never can tell," he answered, and pointed towards a swimming fish.

Something snapped shut as a spray of water hissed up beside us. A little farther along and another clam closed its shell and squirted a spray in alarm. We laughed, for this chap had been asleep and squirted after we passed. Walking softly to one big open shell I prodded the purple flesh inside with a stick. The clam closed instantly, ejecting a spray of water and tightly gripping the stick. Some clams remained open.

These were too far away to hear tis or feel the vibration of our feet, or some sense warned them that danger was not imminent.

"They're poisonous looking things," growled Charlie at one fellow the size of a giant cabbage whose flesh was a vivid pattern of green and purple. "An occasional one grows pearls, milky white things of no value, although a rare one might grow an unusual shape and colour that would be of value to curiosity hunters."

"There'd be no hope for a tiny fish caught between those closing hinges," I remarked.

"No, and very little for the diver when he puts his foot into one of the giants under below."

"The clams don't eat fish?"

"No. They drain their food from minute life in the water. But I've found a "drowned" fish in one of these shells; he was probably speeding away from a pursuing fish and touched the flesh and the clam closed on him."

Lying at the bottom of the pools left by the receding tide were long, uninspiring sausages, black, brown and grey.

"The black fish are all right," said Charlie, pointing to the *beche-de-mer*; "the others are useless. The Chinese won't buy them for soup!"

I wonder if the *beche-de-mer* cutters ever sail this way?"

Yes, but never to the island. They get their *beche-de-mer* from shallow water and the water here goes to great depth straight down from the reef. Away across over the mangroves on the opposite side of the island though there may be shallow water. But those trees would block us from ever seeing a vessel close inshore there."

Some of the pools on the reef surface were six feet deep with water like clear glass; on their inner edges grew fairy gardens of delicately shaped corals and marine growths. Some corals were prettily coloured, some were shaped like dainty ferns and grasses; others resembled ornamental bushes. Broad-leafed plant life, leaves of grotesque colour and pattern and leaf growths as fine as girls' hair were the playground of tiny fish vividly coloured.

These living jewels peeped out from their hiding-places a moment, then swam into the centre of the pool to stare bravely up at us.

"There might be fairy fish down there, where those fern fronds and russet grasses are waving!"

"Yes," growled Charlie. "I've seen chaps like those toy fish playing among a dead man's bones. The niggers swore that the fish that ate his eyes grew eyes of their own that shine like the stars at night . . . And there are more fairies!" He pointed.

Cruising swiftly along the reef edge were numerous black fins. It was the first time I had seen sharks in a school; their shadowy grey bodies and swiftly cruising fins were soon to grow a comparatively familiar sight. Along the reef edge the coral wall was like a precipice, sheering down into deep sea. We peered over and presently could see right down into the depths. Gorgeous coral gardens took shape, and queer things half plant, half animal, and moving things that we could only guess or wonder at. One dark place trellised with waving weeds suggested the entrance to a cavern.

"I could imagine dead men's bones down there," I nodded.

"There's live things a lot worse," answered Charlie. "Come along to the Mound and see if we can find some tin."

A little farther along, we noticed an opening among the mangroves, suggesting the mouth of a small river. As we drew level with the place we could see that at a little distance within the forest the trees closed in, their countless roots walling the space around. These roots were a maze of twisted wood that held up each tree like the ribs of an umbrella. The roots joined the trunk some three feet above the mud, and appeared like miles of writhing snakes all along the forest edge and all through it too, as we found later on. Dark tunnels here and there along the tree wall surrounding this clear place, ran in among the trees over the roots and below the interlocking branches.

"There appear to be creeks running into the forest there; they would be death-traps when the tide comes in."

"They are," said Charlie, staring thoughtfully in among the trees. I wished he would tell me his thoughts, it was such a beautiful day.

But he turned, and walked on up along the reef. Close to the Mound we were forced to wade knee-deep for here a wide creek flowed over the coral and penetrated deep into the mangroves.

"This creek mouth would be a raging torrent when the tide swirls in."

"Yes," said Charlie. "No doubt deep sea fish come racing up here and on into the forest with the tide. There must be some great fights among those mangroves at night."

The Mound proved to be even more unpromising than our two tiny hills, just a squat knob of granite. At its base, where they had toppled upon the reef, were piled up boulders, many of monster size. The soil of this one-time hillock had long since been sucked away by the ever hungry sea. The pate of the Mound was bare rock gleaming in the sunlight. The mangrove side of it, however, was covered by a few inches of decomposed soil, and here existed a handful of undergrowth and dwarf trees.

"Who on earth first brought these trees here?" I asked curiously.

"Are they relics of a growth that existed when this island was part of the mainland, or did land birds carry the seed here?"

"Most likely birds or the sea currents brought the seeds from the mainland. Though the trees could be relics of thousands of years ago."

To our surprise, a few small birds were flitting about here, long beaked birds with yellow breasts whose occasional cheerful whistling gave the only bright side to a depressingly interesting picture.

From the Mound the reef ran east but was not so well defined, for in the near distance the mangroves grew over it to the edge of the sea. Looking back the way we had come, the two little hills seemed growing right up from the mangrove tops. Looking out over the forest from the Mound was to gaze out over a far-spread mass of dark green foliage, the sea invisible on its farther side.

"Well, what do you think of it?" I asked.

"It's all right," answered Charlie soberly. "A bit small maybe. But then, if there is any tin in the place we shall be able to find it all the sooner. Look at that cheeky little bird, I don't believe he's seen a man before."

"He's coming closer to have a good look. And by that perky sideways glance of his head he doesn't think much of us either. I wonder where the little chaps get their water."

"At the well of course. I noticed a dozen there this morning. There's not another drop of fresh water on the island."

"… My God!" Charlie sprang up, his face white.

"What's wrong?"

"I've forgotten my 'scope!"

4

The Scope

Charlie pulled off his flannel. Running right down the side of his body was a fearful scar. It commenced at a gruesome looking hole, the flesh all bunched around it.

"I've got a silver tube in there," he nodded. "Every day I've got to shove the 'scope down it and pour a pint of water and chemicals down. The doctors took away nine feet of my innards in France. I don't treat myself every day as I should, but only when a headache warns me attention is overdue. I felt the headache coming on now as we were talking. I felt it the day we landed, too, but put it down to the booze. Never thought about this! And now I've gone and left the 'scope and chemicals behind in Cooktown!"

"What will happen?"

"I'll swell up and bust!"

"Good heavens!"

Fearfully we stared at one another. Visions of burying this man, of being all alone with a dead man on a tiny island, of having to account to the police afterwards, made me feel sick.

"There's only one thing to do," he frowned thoughtfully, "make a 'scope or perish. Ought to be easy enough to make; it's a simple instrument."

"Come back to camp and start straightaway then. Come along."

But Charlie stood there, staring out to sea.

"I've done it before . . . I've lived on damper and salt beef for six months at a time, then come down to town and forgotten to 'irrigate' except on hops."

"How long do they give you when you forget?" I asked hopefully.

"Forty-eight hours."

"Forty-eight hours! But—you've lasted a week already!"

"More. I was on the hops when we left Cooktown, we were a week on the boat, and this is our second day on the island."

I stared at the man.

"I'm not dead yet," he growled—and a harsh, set look seemed to grow on his jaw.

"What is a 'scope?"

"A tube-shaped thing. It fits right down inside."

"What will you do for chemicals?"

"Sea water might do. It is all chemicals of a sort."

"Come and let us try to make the 'scope immediately then!"

But Charlie picked up his prospecting tools.

"No we won't!" he growled. "I'm going to prospect the Mound thoroughly to-day. It's my own funeral. I forgot the 'scope and I'll put up with it."

"You're mad!"

"Not yet!" he replied grimly, and bent to his digging. Despite all entreaty he kept steadily at work. I couldn't. All the information, all the chance gossip I had heard concerning this man suddenly gathered in concrete form. He had been a "mystery" man of Guy's Hospital; the mystery being that he lived at the time, and kept on living. So intriguing was his case that the medical authorities overseas had made him promise to write them just two words every six months, "still living," while he was able to write. And now here he was cut off from all help. And he had forgotten his 'scope and chemicals. My heavens! How I watched him as he worked, toiling there in the sun, wondering what was happening within that sinewy hairy body.

With only a grumpy spell during the midday meal, he worked hard until the sun was setting, until the tide had surged in and roared out again. As we trudged back along the freshly wet reef he would hardly talk; his face was set in pain that he refused to admit. Our evening meal was miserable.

By fire-light, Charlie set about making his 'scope. With a tomahawk as hammer and pick as anvil, he straightened a pot-hook.

By Jove! We were soon glad of those pot-hooks, short lengths of ordinary fencing wire that we had brought from Cooktown.

Fencing wire is the Australian bushman's friend. I had seen a host of things repaired by, or made from, this wire. I was to see venturesome airmen repair their planes with the rusted strands. But now Charlie was making a medical instrument. He measured the straightened wire with his fingers then chopped it off to the correct length. Thoughtfully he gazed at it, then began gently bending it into shape; he seemed to be making the curve in it by feel—had felt the original being inserted into his side so often, I suppose. In an hour he had fashioned the wire into the correct shape. Holding it to the fire-light he gazed with the expression of an aboriginal expert examining a delicately fashioned spearhead.

"Will it do?"

"I dunno," he replied doubtfully.

He cut a tin bag into strips. These bags are of a specially prepared, very strong canvas. His lean brown fingers twisted a strip around the wire model much as a potter presses a good clay. I kept the fire in a blaze as he bent to its light to sew the canvas shape around the wire. It took two hours to do that sewing. Then he worked the wire from out of the canvas and examined his handiwork, a stiff and perfectly rounded canvas tube with a long curve in it.

"Will it act?"

"I dunno. Might."

Little wavelets tinkled upon the loose corals of the beach.

Charlie hammered flat an empty jam tin, cut off a portion, washed it thoroughly with wet sand, then with the aid of a tomahawk and knife fashioned it into a little funnel. He picked up the billy can and instruments and walked to the beach. When I followed, wishing to help in some way, he walked straight into the water and waded out to a flat rock in the lagoon. Climbing up, he sat down and made a pillow of his shirt. Then, partly twisted to one side, he fumbled about, poking the 'scope down the hole in his side. Stretching out on one side he poked the funnel end into the 'scope and reaching over, filled the billy. He filled the funnel, and lay stretched out there, a black shadow on the big grey rock.

I waited a while, then walked back to the fire and sat there until daylight. It was an awful job trying to keep awake. He came wading ashore at breakfast time, his face deeply lined, his eyes glary.

"It does the job in a sort of way," he growled, "but it's far too slow. I'll have to make an improvement somehow."

"So long as it keeps you alive," I encouraged thankfully, "it does not matter how slow it is." He warmed himself at the fire, morosely refusing breakfast. 1 was too delighted to ruffle him by asking further questions.

A fortnight of bright days, gentle breezes and cool, quiet nights drifted by. Charlie had become his own self again. He was never jovial but when he took an interest in things he was a good, resourceful mate. The fright his physical condition had given me had faded to the confidence that should he become "gassed" again he could use the 'scope. He did so now every day as a matter of fact. The procedure occupied only two hours a day; he used to disappear quietly and I'd make no remarks.

We soon found that what mineral the island contained was buried in the little Peak. In a few days we located it as tiny leaders running across the top of the Peak. These threads of quartz were rich with tin (sometimes combined with wolfram) in small pockets or patches. But the leaders were very thin, from a knife- blade thickness to a quarter of an inch, and in depth they only "lived" to a few feet. Cheerily we began digging them out; it was glorious working up there in the bright sunlight high above a lazy blue sea, the golden grass rustling under every puff of wind. From down behind us where the little trees grew came, nearly always, the cheeky chatter or answering whistle of a bird. Three miles away—it seemed only half a mile, looking down from the Peak— was a little sand-bank on top of a coral reef capped by the dense green of mangroves. This was Coquet Island, and visible like a white pillar above the mangroves was its automatic light. Beyond it were several other dark green clouds on the water that were the mangroves growing on mud bank or coral islet.

"Where are all these wonderful islands a man reads about," I asked one day, "these islands with beautiful mountains and palm- trees and brown-skinned girls swimming in pearly lagoons?"

Charlie pointed towards the mainland: "There are plenty of niggers over there. But the nearest brown-skins are two hundred miles farther north. So are the palms and lagoons and the larger pearl-shell beds. But there are larger islands than these a bit farther north with hills and bush and trees on some—and history, too."

"What sort?"

All sorts. Captain Cook sailed up along here; he named Lizard Island across there because there were lizards on it. Not far north is Restoration Island, the first land Bligh saw after the mutiny of the *Bounty*. There's lots of exploring and pioneer stories all along the coast here, both by land and sea. Later stories, too. Wrecks and blackbirding, quarrels over sandalwood depots and *beche-de-mer* stations, rivalry and grog, 'hell ship' stories, and fights among the blacks and whites and pearling crews. In the days of the pearl-shell rushes, particularly, times were pretty lively in the Coral Sea, some vessels earned a reputation for blood-thirst that a buccaneer would have envied. And some of the islands bred fighting savages who were not afraid to man their big war canoes and tackle the white man. But there's older history than that."

"What is it?"

"Lots. Native legend tells queer stories of wholesale emigrations of strange people, strange races coming to the Great South Land, others hurrying away from it. It might have been all about the time of the break-up between Australia and New Guinea. When that country sank there and left only a chain of connecting islands there must have been some hurry-up movements among whatever populations found themselves being suddenly submerged. Apart from the queer native legends, though, there's Forbes Island. Spaniards are supposed to have been wrecked there in the old galleon days, old-time cannon-balls and other relics have been dug up from the sands. Jardine found treasure trove hundreds of miles farther north, a chest of old-time dollars all cemented together by action of the sea-water and coral. But if you expect to see any brown-skinned girls on this island, you've got as much chance as I have of hopping to Hades."

And Charlie bent to his wolfram digging.

5

Strangers

Every evening we fished for a few hours. Charlie loved fishing; he had brought lines and hooks of all sizes from Cooktown. One line was his pet; it was a rope clothes-line and at the smithy's forge in Cooktown he had made a huge hook, attached by a chain. This was his shark line and looked strong enough to land a whale.

We fished from some boulders that had rolled straight down from the Hill into the water. There must have been a mighty splash when those great boulders came tumbling down to pile into the one deep hole of the lagoon. The water spaces in between the boulders were deep and gloomy, apparently with caverns under be-low, as if other boulders were down there piled on top of one another. We caught some fish every night, a welcome addition to our supply of tinned meats. They were mostly rock cods from five to thirty pounds weight, hefty fellows that pulled sullenly but strongly. Each night, though, we lost lines and hooks.

"There are some big fellows down below," said Charlie with the fisherman's thrill. "I'll land something that will surprise you one of these nights."

Carefully he set larger hooks on stronger lines, using wire, too. Craftily he angled for the fish that were getting away with our hooks. He landed some large fish, but every night lost at least one big hook. Eventually the loss became serious, so I stopped fishing altogether. To the suggestion that we fish where the fish were smaller he stubbornly shook his head, sitting out there in the starlight intent on his line.

"There's a big old man groper under here below," he growled, "and I'm going to land him."

So evening after evening I just looked on and smoked. Gazed up at the stars sometimes, and across the water where it swept before us like a broad river hedged in by mangroves. For there, too, mangroves grew back from the sea edge fringing the lagoon to circle around the Hill and join up with the mangrove forest. That dark tidal river—a river only as it came welling in over the reef and rushed into the island to be walled in by the Hill and the mangroves—was sombrely beautiful. Like dark silver, mysterious in its movements, it came rippling in to swell and climb so treacherously fast up the boulders and mangrove trunks; so full of quiet, eerie noise. The hissing from out in tht silver darkness of baby whirlpools, the soft suckings as it crept rapidly up the boulders, the gurglings and sighs and whisperings as it swirled in among the mangrove roots and, filling their tangled maze, crept up the trunks to suck at their lower branches and leaves. That "river" would deepen and widen our toy lagoon into a real one until it was one broad sheet of rippling silver merging with the sea. Sometimes a streak of brilliant phosphorus would mark its surface as a large fish chased a smaller. When a shoal of vicious fish came harrying other finned occupants of the lagoon the water was spider-webbed with lines of phosphorus as they chased their frantic prey.

But the big old man groper who had his home under below was too full of brute strength to land.

"It's him!" Charlie would exclaim; and I'd wake to see him kneeling down and hanging on to the line which as I grasped it would stretch straight out as if a locomotive were backing slowly at the end. Then the line would come away in our hands—broken. And Charlie would sigh his disappointment.

"I'll get him yet!" he would always growl

And he would produce a still stronger line and a larger hook, and twist more wire from the hook to the line. Then he'd catch one or two big fish with it, but sooner or later the old man groper would take the bait and hook and half the line. I grew watchfully interested in this battle between the man and the fish. That fish had brute wits. He'd play with the bait, nose it, then leave it alone, just to feel Charlie's quivering finger on the line. After a long while he would take the bait within thick lips and slowly swim out. The line would tauten like Charlie's face; then, as he jerked, the fish simply let him jerk the line away. But presently, when he got tired of playing with Charlie, he'd grip the bait and swim with the line under his cavern; and that would be the end of it. And I had a conviction that when Charlie eventually baited his prized shark line, that would be the end of it too. To have pulled up the groper would have meant pulling up the cavern roof.

But the old man groper would not bite at the shark line. Charlie tried his hardest, tempting the unresponsive brute night after night. And each night saw us lose another of our few remaining hooks.

Giant groper are the terror of the reefs where divers go down into the coral gardens seeking pearl-shell. The groper is a massive, hideous brute, nearly all head and mouth armed with terrible teeth that can easily bite off a man's arm. They are bovine, sulky, black and mottled, their strength being measured in hundredweights. Some "old men" from the underwater caverns grow to great size; I remember one caught outside Cooktown that on Bob Walmsley's weighing machine tipped the scale at four hundred-weight. But fish of five hundredweight have been caught.

I have often wondered what the big old man of Howick Island weighs.

While our lines lasted, we caught fish and saved our meat. We had plenty of flour, a fact I mentioned to Charlie.

"I ordered a couple of extra bags," he growled. "You never know."

"That was a lucky forethought anyway. What produced the brainwave?"

"I've been caught before," he answered shortly. "The longer a man lives the more he learns in this country."

But after nearly a month on the island we were rationing our tobacco. To be without tobacco is heart-breaking.

One morning we were down at the camp working on a rough bush kiln in which to burn our tin and wolfram stone. Hard stone is much easier to crush after it has been roasted. We had dug out nearly all the payable stone, and would just have time to separate the tin from it and bag it up before the ketch returned.

It was nearly midday when I picked up the kerosene tin bucket to go for water. I was wood and water Joey; Charlie was cook. He appeared to like cooking; I didn't. Anyway he always did it in a grim sort of way. Thinking cheerfully of the expected approach of the ketch I walked from camp around the base of the Peak towards the well and stood with thumping heart. A man stood, staring at me. He was a man right enough. Suddenly I realized my month's growth of beard. Hat-less and half-clothed, with hair already growing over my forehead, I stared at this clean shaven man in his clean suit. Under his cap his hair was well trimmed. Two other men stood in the grass half way up the Peak, staring down.

"Hullo, who on earth are you?"

"I'm from the lighthouse boat. We're replenishing the oil on the Coquet Island light."

"Oh!"

"We did not know any one was living on this island."

"We're not. We're only here for a few days longer. We didn't dream there was another man within a hundred miles. We're prospecting. Come along and have a yarn with my mate. You're the first visitors we've had."

"It was only by chance we called," he explained as I shouted for Charlie. "As a rule it is impossible to land here on account of the surf and reef. We rowed a dinghy across out of curiosity."

Charlie appeared coming along the track as the two men from the Peak climbed down towards us. Only then did I realize how wild we really looked, for Charlie with his black stubble, his long, iron-grey hair, his deep-set eyes and gaunt, half-clothed figure looked like a man of the woods alongside these clean-shaven strangers.

Charlie acted the host as if he was king of an island. With lively curiosity they accompanied us to camp. They would not accept a drink of tea; a glance at our scanty larder may have decided them.

Charlie insisted that they accept the two fish he had caught the night before, a thirty and twenty pounder cut up and cleaned, hanging in the smoke of the galley. Gladly I accepted a pipe of tobacco, and Charlie added:

"Thanks! It's the only thing we're a bit short of."

"I'm sure the old man would send you some tobacco in return for the fish," volunteered the man I had met first.

"We'd give him all the fish in the ocean if he would," I replied eagerly.

"We'll get you some then. But we'll have to go aboard now; we were only allowed an hour's leave while the crew were refilling the light with oil."

We walked with them back around the base of the Peak towards the broad coral reef now awash under the incoming tide. Their dinghy was tied right up to the mangroves.

They were guardedly curious; we were real Robinson Crusoes to them. Two white men away out here all alone on a tiny speck in the Coral Sea, and without a boat! The seamen could not understand it. But it was a fierce delight to us to talk to men other than ourselves. We tried to hold them, and were sorry when they pushed off promising a speedy return.

"They think we're 'touched'," said Charlie significantly, and tapped his forehead.

I watched them rather longingly as they pulled across to Coquet Island, where a small steamer was anchored.

"How often do they come?" I wondered.

"Once every six or twelve months; it depends on the size of the oil containers. Some automatic lights hold enough oil to last for twelve months."

We stood there, not talking much, watching the dinghy grow smaller as she approached the steamer. It was a three-mile row.

How I hoped the skipper would send the boat's crew ashore again—and with some tobacco. He did; for presently we saw the dinghy heading towards us. We thrilled. This unexpected visit had brightened us up considerably.

But the crew could only stay long enough to hand us several long tins of ship's tobacco and, gift from the gods, some tins of jam and butter, a little sugar, and a pound of tea. The ship was weighing anchor immediately/sailing on up north. The skipper sent an offer to take us off and land us on the mainland if we wished. Charlie laughed the offer away. I smiled thanks less mirthlessly. The ketch was calling back for us any day now and we were returning south. So with a cheery "Goodbye, good luck!" they pushed off and bent to the oars as they battled against the lazy waves that now were commencing to roll in over the reef.

We climbed up on to the Peak to watch them reach the steamer. Immediately they did so the dinghy was hauled aboard and the little vessel steamed away.

"There's something we forgot to ask them,' I said suddenly.

"How soon will they come again?"

"There's something we forgot to ask for far more important than that," he growled.

"What's that?"

"Fish-hooks!"

6

The Big Fish

Even now, I wonder if Charlie has forgiven me. He made a momentary mistake in a business upon which he was, and prided himself to be, an expert. I thoughtlessly corrected the error, and Charlie stood there, dull-faced, imagining he was portrayed in the light of a new chum.

We were burning the tin stone down on the beach near the camp. The kiln was the height of a man, just a "box" of logs with firewood lining the bottom and so arranged that when lighted a draught would blow through. We carried the stone down from the Peak and tipped it into the box until it was full up. Then piled logs on top and set fire to it underneath. It was a slow furnace: we only wanted to "roast" the stone. In a couple of hours this was done; the logs had burned down leaving a pile of whitish-red stones. As this pile was cooling off, we raked it nearly flat with long sticks and threw sea-water over it. The hot stone crackled and split. The mass then was quite easy to crush by simply hammering it with the flat of our picks. As we powdered the stone, the particles of tin and wolfram dropped loose. Next day we sieved the powdered pile and separated the metal by a simple process of "jigging"; using sieves, shaking, and water with gravitation to separate cleanly - the metal from the crushed stone.

shaking, and water with gravitation to s eparate cleanly - the metal from the crushed stone.

The black tin grains showed up richly, in fact, we recovered nearly half a ton of tin and a quarter of a ton of wolfram. Charlie bent over amangrove forest. What on earth was he doing? He was digging, probably trying to locate a reef he had traced down from the side of the Peak. He had dug down and found several reefs. If they had contained tin as did the tiny leaders, we should have been made men. But where he apparently was digging now was on the only flat on the island, a tiny patch of loam that ages of weathering had washed down from the Peak. And, judging by all appearances, there was only dead coral under the loam—no hope of any mineral. In the fading light, he straightened up and walked around the base of the hill towards the camp on the lagoon side of the island. I walked to camp down through the grass whistling to a sleepy fluttering from the tiny clump of trees clinging to the Peak side.

What were you doing down on the flat?" I asked as Charlie bent over the fire. "Digging a garden?" "Yes."

"What! You don't mean it?"

"Yes I do. Some of those sweet potatoes we brought along with us. I put them aside and planted them this afternoon. And I bought some vegetable seeds from Cooktown."

"From Cooktown! Great Scott! Did you really intend to make a garden?"

"If we stayed here, yes. It is the sensible thing to do. Anyway, I always carry seeds in my swag. If a man starts a permanent camp he can grow a vegetable garden, which means he cannot starve."

"But this is not going to be a permanent camp! Anyway, those sweetbuks you planted won't be eatable for three months. We won't be here then, thank goodness!"

"Well, someone else will reap the benefit." "Good heavens! Who would come and live in this God-forsaken hole even if it was a paradise of sweetbuks and pumpkins!"

"I would!" answered Charlie quietly.

I stared as he dropped a pinch of tea in the billy, then lifted it off. He cut a hunk of damper and reached for some fried fish. Our dripping was getting very low; it was too precious to use as butter now.

"You are joking, Charlie."

"No."

I reached for the damper and my share of fish and chewed away, staring at the evening chasing its shadows across the un-flowing waters of the lagoon. Then: "You can't be in earnest Charlie! For a man to live alone on this isolated speck of coral, granite and mud is unbelievable. Just the wide sky by day.

At night the everlasting breakers on the reef. His only companions a few half-starved birds fluttering to the well to drink. Robinson Crusoe was never so lonely. He had a large island, a blackfellow and a parrot for company. Here you would have—nothing!" Well, what about it?"

"Heavens, man, where's your sense of companionship? Don't you want to see other people, to hear them talk? In the loneliest part of the bush you can jump on a horse and in a week or two reach a town or camp. Here you would be dependent on often unfavourable winds and a passing boat that couldn't or wouldn't call. You probably would not see a fellow man once in twelve months. Not in years, unless it was for the yearly visit of that light-house boat. And it could not land even then if the weather was rough."

"Well!"

"Well! Don't you ever want to see towns again—see other men and hear them talk?" "No! You can keep your hotbeds of disease and squalor, your wretched picture shows and artificial people. What has the world done for me? Nothing but bullocking toil to earn a crust! And all your 'human companionship' thinks of is to take the other fellow down if he has money, and kick him into the gutter if he hasn't. The world has no time for me and I've got no time for the world. To hell with the world!"

That night, sitting out on the big black rock, Charlie fished the night through and didn't catch a fish. The old man groper came and took two hooks.

We knew instantly it was the old man by the way he swam out with the tautening line, then without the least haste or flurry turned and swam against our strength deeper down under the rocks and calmly broke the line. His great jaws must have been studded with hooks, but the monstrous mouth would hardly feel such prickles.

Charlie fished grimly. We had hardly spoken since the evening meal. I wished the ketch would come. Charlie, by all the signs, was accumulating "gas" again. I longed to ask if he had used the 'scope that day, but dared not. Crouched there with the line be-tween his fingers, his eyes glaring at the water, he evidently was awaiting some such question as he was await-ing the bite of the fish. But the old man groper would not bite at the shark line although it was baited so temptingly. Charlie again and again manoeuvred the bait to "swim" just before where he judged the mouth of the cavern to be. But the big fish ignored the line.

We were on our last few hooks now. They had served their purpose and saved our tins of meat. With that and the extra flour and several other extras Charlie's forethought had ordered, together with the little gifts from the lighthouse steamer, we had sufficient to last until the ketch arrived. The tin and wolfram was all bagged and lying ready by the beach. It would mean only a matter of moments for us to pull down the tent and pack up once we sighted the ketch. There was nothing to do but wait.

It was perishingly cold there on the rock. I jumped from boulder to boulder, then walked on the mangrove roots above water to the shore for the blanket.

Returning I rolled up in the blanket beside the silently fishing Charlie, gazed up at the sky and—fell asleep.

Next morning, Charlie was sitting hunched up by the campfire, his eyes bloodshot, his mouth sullen. He snarled when I inquired if I could do anything for him.

7

The Sand-Flies

That night Charlie lost our three remaining hooks—through no fault of his. A very high tide came flooding in until the water not only covered the mangrove roots and trunks but crept up to the lower branches. That tide hissed in like a great river in flood with its banks soon under water that swirled away among the trees. Apprehensively I gazed at the black mangrove tops that were the shore, for between us and them swept hurrying water. Out in the starlight was the hissing of big fish sweeping in over the reef and lashing the water as they chased frantic prey. Presently our boulder was only six inches above water, while a boulder that usually, stood like a house farther out-stream loomed barely seven feet above the swirling current. A tree, washed from the distant mainland, came swimming silently into the flooded l agoon. W ith a j arring t hreat a b ranch scraped up over the boulder and we had to push desperately against it or be pushed off.

"With all the wide ocean to sail on," grunted Charlie as we strained against the quivering branches, "this, tree must come from a continent and cross a sea to scrape against two men on a rock by an island!"

Charlie had immediately pulled up his prized shark line as the submerged tree loomed up from the dark at our feet. I had hauled on the other line; but it caught in the branches and, despite Charlie's frantic efforts, as the big tree slipped away into the darkness it carried the hook with it. Charlie was upset. Those last few hooks had grown surprisingly precious to him. Growling at luck, he re-baited the shark line and threw it over. An hour passed without a bite though big fish leapt and popped all around us. Charlie sprang up and baiting his last line but one, threw it in. It was seized immediately as a swarm of sharks sped by; one big fellow swerved to the rock and the splash as he sheered off lapped our feet. Charlie's line snapped and he swore as he grabbed for the shark line. Not a bite, though foam spurted up as big fins hissed through the water all around us for ten lively minutes. We gazed at silvered bodies trailing brilliant phosphorus as they sped past and around the rock. Beautiful glimpses of a fiercely virile life in a world not our own. How they would have torn a man to pieces if he had slipped in! But not a fish of any sort bit at the bait on Charlie's shark line.

By and by the night quietened, as it always does when the tide is at the full and no wind disturbs the waters. Charlie's big line pulled slowly out, I caught the excitement in his crouching figure as he stiffened quiet as a statue. The line lifted and straightened right out. Charlie keeping a gentle pressure on it, let it slowly slide through his fingers. He was angling for the old man groper, he daren't tug lest the big fellow were merely nosing the bait. I crept up beside him. The line kept going straight out in a long, steady pull. Then Charlie tugged viciously.

"He's on!" he shouted as he jumped up. I grasped the line and we pulled. The line came in as if a sack of coal were at the end, then it pulled down through the water at our feet.

"He's going into the hole," called Charlie desperately and pulled in the line hand over hand. But the brute remained stuck down there, around a corner of the rock I suppose. We couldn't budge him. For ten minutes we pulled the line at different angles, trying to get his jaw around. Then the line slackened, to pull steadily again as the big fish swam out into the lagoon.

"Play him!" cried Charlie as he eased the line. "He's too big to pull in, we'll have to drown him!" The line went out to nearly its limit.

Charlie in alarm began hanging on. I hung too; but the line just pulled out as if a draught- horse was on it. Despite Charlie's efforts as it dragged to the limit the line finally took the strain where it was fastened to the rock. It stretched a moment thus, then parted and was gone.

About the middle of the next night I sat up sleepily, subconsciously wondering at the intense silence. The usual rumbling on the reef was now hushed to a whispering croon. The sea breeze had completely died away, leaving us in a motionless world. But there was a shrill, insistent buzzing, bringing a hot sense of burning face and arms. I sprang up among a swarm of sand-flies. Shaking head and brushing hands were futile, as well try to brush away, the sands of the sea. The insects filled nose and eyes and ears.

Charlie was already bending over a fire and the chocolate-coloured wood he was using quickly filled the tent with a floating, perfumed smoke.

"Thank heaven for that," I breathed. "It's lucky you found that wood. Where did you get it?"

Almost immediately, the sand-flies vanished.

"It's drift-wood from the mainland, I've used this stuff before. I noticed this piece lying among the mangroves when we landed, and I marked the spot."

"Good job you did; My arms and face feel burning raw. I've never experienced sand-flies so thick before."

"I have. But this is only a small island. They've got no room to spread out. They're hungry."

"What on earth brought the pests?"

"They just come."

"I wish that ketch would come!" I said irritably. "I wonder what is keeping the skipper. He is overdue, and the wind is (or was) in our favour."

Charlie didn't answer.

All the remainder of the night we were forced to sit up tending the fire, half choking in the heavy smoke. At last the longed for daylight arrived. Thankfully I stepped out of the tent—and jumped straight back, attacked by swarms of insects. Slapping at face and arms I buried my head in the smoke.

Then followed three weeks of sheer misery. Not the faintest breath of wind, the sea a vast plate of shining glass, the sun's rays reflected from the granite rocks in a shimmering, burning heat. Days and nights a ceaseless, shrilling misery. We never had pipe or cigarette out of our mouths. I took to swathing face and arms against the sand-flies and then, like a living mummy, climbed the Peak and gazed out to sea in sweating misery for hours. The flies were not so bad up on the Peak. A breath of air would come; sometimes then it was joy to whip off the rags and stand bathing the face in coolness. The breath would die again to an intense silence, almost immediately broken by the shrill of the flies swarming back.

That was an awful silence under the sun's glare. Even the tide came in silently over the reef; the few birds were silent. Every day as I rushed down to the well for water they would merely hop up on to the mangrove branches and wait for me to go. From the Peak, day by day, never a sail was visible.

Charlie made only one comment.

"Don't be a fool. The ketch can't come while this calm is on. And the flies won't go either."

The days and night crawled by; days that dragged our spirits down to zero and brought us face to face with starvation.

"It's the last tin!" said Charlie gruffly one night.

Something in his tone made me stare. Our last tin of meat! With the misery of the sand-flies these last few weeks I had not thought of the dwindling food-supply. Charlie reached for a tobacco tin, one of the large ones given us by the lighthouse crew. It was half empty. He emptied it on to a board and with a knife carefully divided the little heap of precious weed.

"And there's the last of the tobacco," he growled. "Take your share!"

I glanced around the tent. There was a full fifty-pound bag of flour remaining. We could not starve until that was done, anyway. Now I cursed the loss of the fish-hooks. And realized why Charlie this last month past had so carefully saved the used-up tea leaves from the billy can. We had long since run out of milk and sugar. From now on, it would be rough living.

That brought a sudden thought. How would Charlie's insides work, now that we had to live on flour alone? I stared glumly at the two little heaps of tobacco. If Dick and I had been alone on an island we would never have divided the tobacco, we would just have smoked it, then sworn a bit and laughed a lot.

Outside the tent was the shrilling of the flies, baffled by the smoke from the chocolate-coloured wood. We had something to be thankful for—Charlie recognizing that wood.

We ate our meal in silence—had done so frequently lately.

8

The Fish Spear

A few days later we were meat hungry. A famishing feeling; it gnaws inside a man when he has lived a few days on damper alone.

One morning Charlie brought a long galley hook into the tent. He straightened the wire, then chopped it into four pieces each about eighteen inches long. Each of these in turn he laid on the flat of the axe and carefully straightened by taps with the hammer. I looked on moodily until he began to file a point on each piece of wire. "A fish spear!" I thought with quickening interest. "A fat lot of fish he'll spear!" But hunger sharpens a man's wits. Charlie slipped out to the galley and came back with a bamboo rod. Brushing the flies off face and wrist as he dived into the smoke again, he sat back and began to fit the wire prongs to the end of the rod. Carefully he placed each prong in such a position that it jutted outward from the rod, and the four prongs commanded as broad an area as possible without detracting from their strength. How often I had sat at a campfire and watched an aboriginal spear maker fashioning his weapon with scientific accuracy! How I now wished I had persuaded them to train me in the use of these weapons. Carefully and firmly Charlie began binding the prongs on to the rod, using a broken-off piece of fishing line. Concentrated on the job, his deep-set eyes were screwed up as his brown fingers craftily tightened the binding. It was not the first spear he had made and I grew a sudden hungry confidence.

"Coming?" he asked as he took off his boots. We both wore boots now, with rags bandaged around them and the bottoms of our trouser legs, to keep out the sand-flies.

"Are you going into the mangroves?" I asked incredulously.

"Yes."

"But you'll have to walk barefooted through the mud, you'll be eaten to death!"

"No I won't."

"Why not try the lagoon? At least it is open water."

"When you can spear a fish in open water," he answered, "you will have learnt something the niggers know. Coming?"

"No I'm not!"

Charlie walked out of the tent without another word.

Several hours later he returned with two fine cod, about three pounds' weight each. His wrists and ankles were red from sand-fly bites, his eyelids inflamed. But those fat fish!

"How on earth did you get them?" I called as I ran out to the galley to blaze up the fire. "I never knew that fish stopped in the mangroves after the tide went out!"

"In the mangroves are creeks that have an inlet and outlet to the tide," he answered. "If there is feed in such a creek it generally swarms with fish when the tide goes out. The creeks twist in and out among the roots of the mangroves. As the tide rushes out through the channels it leaves the mangroves bare, but in some creeks there are always pools of still water left. Various fish hide here among the mangrove roots, and wait for the high tide to come in again so that they can swim out among the mangroves for food. Others stay in the mangrove pools all the time. Now, you have seen me make this spear, and I've told you where the fish are. For the future, do your own fishing. I do mine."

That meal was eaten in silence, the sauce all taken out of it.

Next morning, while Charlie finished the scant remains of yesterday's fish, I made a fish spear. It was a silent job, but one in which I learnt a lot.

Although I had actually lived and wandered amongst the blacks I found how little I really knew of the practical making and use of their most ordinary tools of subsistence. Any native would have laughed hilariously at that spear, but I felt ashamedly proud of the clumsy thing, and felt an urge to hurry to use it.

Charlie had gone inland into the mangroves from the front of the tent, turning left, around the little Hill. For some reason I hurried down towards the well at the back of the camp and entered the mangrove forest in nearly the opposite direction. Immediately, the sand-flies attached themselves in shrilling millions despite the muffling of rag around the face. But in the gloom of the mangroves there was a coolness and a waiting stillness as I pushed cautiously farther in. It was a weird sort of place for a man to venture in alone for the first time. In ages past our hairy ancestors have hunted in similar places, and their experiences have left a heritage of uneasiness in us. In more confident circumstances I had crossed through mangrove swamps fringing the coast. But this place was a sea swamp in a forest and a man felt so much alone—and not too sure what he was to do or look for. Where on earth could I find a creek in this maze?

Impossible to see more than a few yards in any direction, for the trees grew separated only by their interlocking roots. Mostly these grew so thickly up out of the mud that it was easiest to walk on them by stepping from one to the other, the spear in one hand, the other outstretched to seek balance against the trunks. And thus the sand-flies got in torturing work every moment that a man ceased slapping his feet.

In twenty minutes the feet and wrists felt like raw meat, burning intolerably. I jumped down into some thick blue mud and buried my feet to the knees. The cool relief was immense. I smeared the gluey mud thickly over face and wrists and in relief climbed up on to the roots again. Just overhead were the branches roofed densely with dark green foliage, shutting out the sky. Occasionally, a startling "plop!" broke the stillness as a long, torpedo-shaped mangrove seed speared down into the mud. Unhealthily coloured bubbles like an oil film spilt on a dirty road were rising slowly up from some of the mud pools. It might have been gas of decaying vegetable matter or perhaps the effervescence caused by some beast burrowing in his hole below. Queer gurglings came from goodness knows where.

Those deceptive roots soon had me reaching out and testing each gingerly by foot. Occasionally one would snap under the weight and drop me floundering in the ooze. Even if a man could find a creek in such a hole as this how on earth could he find room to throw a spear!

At last there came the gleam of water ahead, down in among the roots, a quickening sight. A chain of little water pools, very still and crystal clear, a mangrove creek—this in a big swamp set in the heart of an enormous coral reef. The roots, like low, trellised walls, were the creek banks. The mangrove trunks innumerable were set in low, gloomy space, the branches meeting above so that their leaves formed a roof-like canopy.

Crouching upon the roots I gazed down with a quick eagerness. The sand grains on the shallow bottom were perfectly distinct; it was possible to see clearly in among the roots on either side. Where the water lay among them their red and green and mottled bark was magnified; queer shells with crawly things in them were moving very slowly upon sand or root. But there was not one solitary fish in all the pool. That was keen disappointment. Leaning farther out over the roots to see plainer, I stabbed the spear haft in the water for a support. "Plop—splash!" a big fish darted from the roots at my very feet. In trembling surprise I watched the water corrugate in ripples as two other fish darted from somewhere. No sight of the fish, only the ripples sweeping out among the roots. Silently the pool silvered over again. Only two feet deep, a clear coral-sand bottom, but not a sign of a fish! They must have sped into the tangle of half-submerged roots. Like a cat seeking a mouse I began stepping over the roots around the edges of the pool, peering into the pool and down among the roots, all keyed up with excitement, quite lost to the world, hardly even noticing the sand-flies. But no sign of a fish. Pausing to think a while, I jabbed the spear half down in among the roots, and stared, listening. Not a movement. And the only sound "plop!" as a mangrove seed dropped into mud away within the forest. I stepped on to farther roots and splashed the spear half down again. At the third try a fish sped across the pool, rippling it merrily.

It was a great discovery. There really were plenty of fish in this tiny pool—in among the roots. The only thing to do now was to find them. For an hour I stepped crouching along those roots, and back along them and back along them again. At rare intervals a fish darted away from directly below. A quickening eye caught a ripple several times, but never sight of a real fish.

By now driven half-crazy by sand-flies, I thought longingly of the relief-giving smoke in the tent. But the imperative demands of hunger would brook no defeat, and besides there was the thought of returning to the camp with no fish—and the silence of Charlie!

I sat on a bunch of roots for another half-hour, hands ceaselessly brushing at the sand-flies, eyes staring down into the water between the roots. Surely there could be nothing wrong with those eyes; they were keen eyes. No, the sparkle of the tiniest grains of sand down there was quite distinguishable. Could the fish actually dive into the sand on the pool bottom, or into the mud among the roots? Staring, I suddenly imagined a root moved. It was only a flake of bark from a mangrove root, just barely swaying to and fro in the water. No, a tiny leaf it was, tinged a brown colour, stuck against a mangrove root. But the tide had gone out. There should be no movement at all in the water—

How the old heart thumped! That leaf was really the side fin of a fish. My eyes followed its gentle pulsing into the mottled body of a fine fat cod and thrilled to distinguish it thus gradually as the body of a fish leaning against a root, to stare at that shadowy shape definitely taking form right to its big head, the big gills faintly but distinctly opening and closing, two owlish, protruding eyes staring straight up into mine.

With trembling hand I lifted the spear, slowly bringing the prongs to bear while sliding them into the water directly above the fish.

I stared into its eyes; it stared into mine— then I lunged down.

A foam, a swirl, a splash of tail, the pool in a hundred ripples—the fish gone. In bewilderment I stared down believing it could not be possible to have missed the fish. But the prongs of the spear were deeply embedded in an underwater root.

As I tugged miserably at the spear, the haft came away in my hands, the wire prongs stayed embedded in the roots. Jumping down into the water I furiously wrenched them out. Fish darted past in frightened haste, one brushed my feet—the place was alive with fish. Clambering up on to the roots I hastily bound the prongs on again, warm triumph quickly gaining over baulked anger. I knew how to look for fish now.

Stepping over the roots, peering between the interlacing maze below water, peering along each root until it joined or was criss-crossed by another root, disappointed at false alarms by mottled bark on sombre green, sometimes spotting a fish that proved merely a fish-shaped root, it was a long time before I distinguished another tell-tale fin. Yes, the movement of a fin gently pulsing on a fish whose body was otherwise indistinguishable where its shape merged against a dark green root.

Making deadly sure this time, I lunged again. With a swirl the fish was gone.

I was utterly bewildered, could not imagine how it was possible to miss a fish but two feet under water. Through that baffled disappointment gradually grew a sense of an eerie, persistent gurgling growing from all around. The tide was coming in—it had arrived noiselessly, but was now swiftly sucking its way among the roots. The pool had grown appreciably deeper, the water had spread right out among the roots! A big fish came racing up the creek where water had not been before.

In quick fright I sped to hasten slowly back over the roots. To be caught in the maelstrom this place must be when the tide was in would be a nightmare indeed.

9

Secrets of the Mangrove Forest

Next morning early, the outgoing tide saw me creeping into the mangroves, meat hungry, eager, confident. Savagely so. Knowing now in which direction to seek a creek and progressing faster in a better understanding of how to walk upon the roots—above all, knowing how to look for the fish. Arid I *must* learn how to spear them.

At first peep of the pool, there was a dying ripple that faded into a pool of glass as I gazed. Some leisurely fish had just crossed. There was movement in the centre of the pool, too, right on the white bottom, a green crab large as a saucer walking quickly sideways across to the sheltering roots, his nippers half erect as if expecting attack by a fish.

None made a rush, though I held the spear ready. That pool, in its silence and gloom, might have been deep in some moonlit cavern where, nothing lived save things of the water and mud.

It was some time before I located the fin of the first fish. I speared and missed and the pool broke with his fleeing ripples. When it quietened, I stepped like an anxious cat among the mangroves and up over the roots.

To creep so above numbers of fish and not know how to see and spear them was heart-breaking.

At last the magnetic attraction of a thing keenly sought brought my eyes staring straight down into the glassy, goggle eyes of a cod. He waited there directly below while I stealthily brought the spear to bear with absolute certainty. As its four points just tipped the surface the water sucked up to them. He did not even quiver to the movement, his unwinking eyes just glared up, his gills slowly pulsing, his big snub snout lying close against the root. Slowly, trying to keep the arm from trembling, I lowered the prongs farther into the water until they seemed almost touching the fish, then lunged. A great splash, the feel of the spear deeply embedded, a laughing warmth of triumph. Not until the last ripple had died away and all was clear would I really believe the spear was embedded in the roots alone.

It was bewildering. I had hunted with natives when they speared fish, in river, lagoon, or the sea edge. They seldom had trees to guard against there, but then they had to throw a long way and at swimming fish too, at the ripples (as I thought then). But here I crouched above a pool barely three feet deep and big fish would lie there absolutely moveless while I took the most accurate aim—and missed.

The sand-flies allowed no brooding over disappointment; the cursed things were a constant misery of stinging bites in nostrils, ears, eyes, any part that could not be plastered with mud.

The fish remained out of sight. Thinking that in some other pool they would be undisturbed and possibly easier to see, I moved along. At both ends of this pool the roots closed in to a narrow channel of mud—-no sand or water. I jumped down and squelched slowly up through the mud. It was really a twisting channel way, hedged on either side by roots. Presently, there came the delightful gleam of water ahead, another pool—and fish were in it! But again I missed. All a man's canny manoeuvring, his hungry caution, his fear of the tide rushing in before securing something to eat, were in vain. And might have been so for a further week but for that element "Luck"—in this case doing the right thing in what was apparently the wrong way. As a big white cod came swimming leisurely beneath I lunged desperately downwards, certain the spear would not reach within a foot of his tail. Instantly the spear was almost wrenched away as in laughing glee I kept my weight hard down on the haft: I had speared my first fish! And how he kicked and wrenched and splashed! Holding the spear firmly I reached one hand down for his head, got a firm grip of the big gills, pulled out the spear and lifted the prize out of the water.

Instantly the big cod doubled up then straightened taut like a released steel trap, his needle-sharp teeth lacerating my fingers. Another powerful jerk and he splashed the water and was gone.

The creek had crept into a shiny, snaky line, it was a live thing imperceptibly growing and snaking along and spreading. Then came the whisperings, then gurglings and eerie sounds deep in among the mangroves before, in haste, I sighted the next fish. Wits driven by necessity were working sharply. That last fish had been speared when I felt certain the thrust would land a foot behind its tail! That might account for missing the others. Perhaps there was something deceptive in the water; the fish might not be where it appeared to be!

The fellow visible now was a big flat fish with a tiny tail. Just another shot before the tide swirled in. I aimed carefully a foot length *behind* the fish, and lunged down. With intense delight I felt its struggling plunges vibrating the spear, as, leaping into the water, I pressed the haft, pinning the fish to the bottom. The body twisted up as with a resounding "flop" the fish was gone, carrying the spear prongs with him.

A six-inch wave of water came hurrying straight up the creek, its flanks behind spreading out among the roots right and left. Across mud flats, unseen among the trees, little rushing waves were spreading with a growing, sucking sound. In wrathful misery I hurried away through the mangrove-trees chased by the tide. Charlie was at the camp just sitting down to a fat meal of fish. He merely kept on eating with no greeting and no invitation. I mixed up some flour and water, kneaded it into a johnny-cake and slung it on the coals. Then took a long galley hook and began making another spear. But a much more careful, more efficient job this was. I turned the johnny-cake and when it was cooked brushed the charcoal off it and ate the leathery stuff, washing it down with the last of my share of the tea, the leaves of which had been brewed several times before. Then, in a much better temper, I turned again to the spear, and worked into it a sort of eager triumph, thinking eagerly of the morrow. For now I knew how to detect, and to aim and to thrust to spear a fish. As to holding and securing him when once impaled, well—that would solve itself. Anyway, all the fish could not be, so big and strong and slimy as those already speared.

Sundown was coming before that spear was finished. A very poor spear from an aboriginal point of view. Still, it was a strong spear, a spear that would hold its prey. The lessons of failure and fright of hunger were woven into that weapon. I balanced it and walked down towards the well, wishing it were next day with the tide out. It was starting to drift out now but would not leave the mangroves dry until long after dark. Still, there being nothing else to do and nowhere else to go, some instinct even against the sand-flies urged me towards the partially exposed reef.

Near the edge, a shoal of brilliantly hued parrot-fish were racing home. They were very beautiful, big and fat too. I longed for a throw, but it was utterly hopeless. It meant a throw not a jab, and even if a fish were impaled he would race into deep water and the spear would be lost. Also, there were some ominous black fins hovering near the edge of the deep water.

Something slithered as I stood stock-still with tingling feet. A green crab the size of a small dinner plate, champing enormous claws, scampered from a shallow pool and made straight for the mangroves. I was after it instantly, stabbing again and again. With almost human agility it dodged, clashing its great nippers at the quick spear prongs. It fought for its life, dodging with incredible cunning, and actually reached the mangroves with me stabbing now in a wild despair. It was slithering across a gnarled root when a final lunge drove the four prongs through the hard shell back. In foolish delight I stooped, but those nippers clashed like castanets a hairbreadth below my fingers. In a flash memory told how natives manipulate giant crabs. As I gingerly reached behind the thing's head, although impaled, it tried desperately to reach its claws over its back. But it can only reach a certain distance. One sharp, sideways jerk and each claw in turn was detached from its body. This prize, this meal was secure. Although intensely delighted, I looked back and went carefully over every detail of the little drama. Necessity is a painstaking teacher.

From the exposed reef where it had been fishing, that crab had fought its way back to the mangroves and almost entered a hole dug in the coral, under the mangrove roots—a surprising hole, like a young rabbit burrow. There was a ledge of dead coral here, in places three feet high, running along the inland reef edge of the mangrove roots. Those claws must be of enormous power to dig holes in stone. Dead coral is really hard, brittle stone.

At a slithering rattle I wheeled around to see a large blue crab diving sideways into another hole. A delightful sight. There appeared to be a number of holes dug in the coral just above high water mark. The hunting lust fairly surged within me as I peered about. Poking half way out of the mouths of their holes several big crabs were cautiously watching as I wheeled around at another rattling and saw five whopper crabs scuttling in alarm for their burrows. As I sprang towards them the hard shell of their bodies rattled over the loose corals. In a few minutes I'd speared several big chaps and stood there with spear upraised glaring around for others, just wild with the successful hunt lust. All thoughts of evening, of everything, were entirely blotted out. But crabs possess cunning or instinct; they vanished, except one belated chap scuttling down his burrow. And night had come in earnest.

That was a glorious meal. I offered Charlie a share. When he just scowled and turned his head away, I laughed. Fortunately I'd seen the aboriginals cooking crabs and knew the poisonous part to throw away. That meal was truly delicious, the huge claws full of sweet meat. Always afterwards, the crabs were our meat; the fish were fish.

10

The King Tides

Stretching luxuriously out on the bank I prepared to enjoy the very last smoke of tobacco. Charlie would smoke longer; he was denying himself just for the pleasure of smoking during the long nights to come when I should have no tobacco. Not that he would have any extra tobacco; he had been scrupulously fair and had divided the last that was left. But his bushcraft would give him a smoke apart from that. He was saving and drying the tea leaves after the last possible sip of tea had been stewed out of them; he was collecting shreds of some kind of seaweed too and drying them with the tea leaves. I was not supposed to know, but I did. Two men on a tiny island can know quite a lot of one another's doings without saying anything about it. In a number of ways he seemed to be regarding our stay on the island as of long duration, regardless of the fact that the ketch must come and pick us up when the wind came.

But I was in a wonderful humour, felt absolutely independent. And thrilled with a triumph of prehistoric man. I knew how to find fish and spear them; knew where the big crabs were. I could not starve.

Feeling like a good yarn, I tried to make friends with Charlie, but was not hurt much when he hardly growled an answer. Now and again he would turn from his bunk to poke a stick of the chocolate wood closer in to its fellows, so that always a wisp of perfumed smoke was slowly ascending to keep "life" in the mist that constantly filled the closed-in tent. We were forced to keep that tent practically sealed. Outside, through the otherwise silent night, came the ceaseless shrill of the sand-flies. "How's the 'scope working?"

"All right."

"How much longer will this calm last?" "How the hell do I know?"

I smoked that pipe down to the very charcoal in the wood, blowing the last ghostly whiff up into the scented smoke. That smoke used to rise while slowly spreading out right to the ridge-pole and hover there as it thinned out before slowly creeping as vapour back down the sides of the tent. That's what we called "live" smoke, when it would rise and hover. When it sank back down the sides of the tent to fade away towards the floor we called it "dead" smoke. We had learnt how to regulate the smouldering sticks now so that a minimum smoke coil allowed us to breathe in some comfort while its pungency was just sufficient to keep out the sand-flies. Evidently the peculiarly penetrating and pungent scent from the smoke exerted a very powerful effect upon the insect devils' breathing apparatus. The nights in the tent were stifling. Outside, but for that weird shrill from countless billions of insects, there was an utter silence of sky, sea, and island.

"I've never even heard of such a plague of sand-flies before. Where do they come from?"

"The sand. Some say they breed in the man-groves. Then, when a wind comes, they are swept for miles up or down the coast and land on the nearest place handy when the wind drops."

"I wish these had dropped into the sea! Just as well there's a limit to insect hosts or they'd eat out nations."

"I've known a plague of caterpillars eat out a tribe's hunting-grounds," said Charlie. "They came and ate every blade of grass, even the fallen leaves from the trees. It was the strangest thing. They ate the country enclosed in that particular tribal area to the last blade of grass, then vanished. All the game cleared out into the surrounding country. It was a rough circle of country, bounded by three other tribes. The edges of that circle were green timber and grass. Inside, it was just bare earth. The niggers had to follow the game or starve. But wherever they turned towards the grass country they were met by hostile spearmen. Witch-doctors had spread the word that the tribe was accursed, that a great devil-devil had spread the plague amongst them and that if any member of that tribe was allowed hunt on any other tribes' ground, the caterpillars would come there too."

"What happened?"

"The tribe was wiped out."

Charlie would not talk any more; still, it had been an agreeable ending to a great day. I dozed, watching Charlie morosely arranging the sticks of wood for the night. After several nights the ends would smoulder so far away from one another that they would die out. Charlie being the lighter sleeper, always woke up first. Night after night I had half awakened with a drowsy grunt knowing more than seeing Charlie bending over the fire-sticks. With the relief-giving smoke the devilish tormentors would disappear and sleep come again.

But for the recurrent after effects of that awful wound in his side, Charlie would have been a splendid mate. The poor wretch was suffering a lot of pain but was cracking hardy. All very well for these tough he-men; for myself, I've always appreciated a little sympathy. A man with a recurrent hurt like Charlie's should never have left civilization and the prompt medical treatment available there. But then, a man used to wandering in the wild places, free and untrammelled, and glorying in being independent of civilization, would break his heart if chained to the very thing he prided himself he could live without.

I fell asleep—and jumped out of my bunk hours later with face and arms covered with stinging insects, nostrils, lips, ears, eyelids burning from their bites. Frantically rubbing face and neck, I groped for the matches. Charlie was snoring brokenly; his insides would be bad to-morrow. What caused him to sleep so soundly to-night?

And the fire ... I struck a match ... It was beside Charlie, against his side of the tent; and his bunk was so shielded by a shirt and bag that the smoke was thrown back and floated only over him! The supply of perfumed wood was gone!

The match burned right down. I ran out into the night, scrambled about the beach for wood and got a taste of what it feels like to be eaten alive. As I ran madly back into the tent the shrilling blanket of insects came too, driving me cursing mad as I lashed tight the tent door. Thrashing arms and face and neck I almost howled before that fire kindled into flames, I could have torn Charlie limb from limb. The fire gave out very little smoke; it meant another rush to the beach and frantic tearing down of a branch to rush back and throw green leaves on the fire. That smoke filled our eyes and nostrils and throats and almost smothered us. It was a night of utter wretchedness relieved only by the sweet knowledge that Charlie must suffer too.

When, at long last, dawn came I searched the little beach around the lagoon in vain for more of the chocolate-coloured wood. There was not a chip. But I found a dry, pulpy log of softwood, carried it back to camp and threw it by my side of the tent.

Then I snatched up the spear and went fishing for breakfast. And got two. I speared them savagely and surely, then jumped into the water, keeping the weight on the haft but not pushing the prongs through — while the fish was struggling. When he stretched out gasping a sudden firm pressure on the haft sent the prongs through deep into the sand. Then, still holding the haft, I bent down and pushed one hand under the fish until the fingers gripped the prong points, held these tightly and lifted spear and fish and all.

As the days passed by, experience made expert in the essential details: where to expect and how to detect a fish; how to spear and lift him by the spear, then flip him out among the mangroves or bend down and grip him by the gills; how to slip him with others along a spiked stick and so carry them easily hitched to the belt. And a way of breathing came, frequent quick little snorting breaths that drove the sand flies from the nostrils when they were very bad.

The tides now were very big, flooding in higher and higher till a morning came when only the tops of the mangrove forest were above water. That day we watched the water come creeping out of the mangroves and up to suck at the grass on the little flat. This silent blow from the sea seemed the deliberate threat of an overwhelming enemy, for it almost robbed us of food-supply: not only was the forest submerged, but the great reef was under many feet of water. The tides were so big that they practically remained stationary; for days the mangroves were swamped and as this left no creeks in which the fish could concentrate, we couldn't fish. The crabs solved the problem; for they came pouring out of the mangroves when the rising waters brought them easy foods not only from the sea but from the island. Their burrows now being feet under water, the crabs were hard to locate; for they spread out scouting in the shallow water over the land, having the time of their lives as each new tide level enabled them to forage still farther for insects in the grass. We waded spear in hand among the grass tufts seeking the gleam in the brilliant sunlight of big blue or purple or green shell that should betray the adventurous crab. Wonderful forests, rich with new and rarely attainable foods, those grasses must have appeared to the crabs.

Charlie would not spear in my crab colony; he wandered in the opposite direction, along the mangroves from the lagoon edge in front of the camp. The waters from the mangrove forest and the lagoon were now meeting. Charlie watched for any stray crab that ventured into the grass from the lagoon side. He would have nothing to do with my crab colony.

One morning we awoke to find the grasses at the base of the Hill and Peak all under water, only the taller tufts showing here and there. Sun and sky were hot and brazen; we could see shell-fish and quaint sea insects crawling busily among the roots of the grasses. There was a deathly stillness over the island; the tortured birds had hardly called at all since the sand-flies came, but to-day marked the first day of utter silence. Not even a leaf stirred, everything was given up to things of the water. Our only dry ground was microscopic now. We should have realized this menace of the King tides; but the strange environment, the torture of the sand flies, and the longing for a wind to break the calm had, kept' all thoughts of anything else from our heads. The bloodshot eyes of Charlie, the grim, stubbornly closed mouth, told that he was suffering' pain too much to safeguard against anything at all.

It was when Charlie came wading back from the well that an awful feeling gripped me. I knew. Charlie said nothing; as he passed the galley fire-place his face was deeply drawn. He walked heavily into the tent and stretched out on his bunk. I went up the tiny rise on which the camp was built, then down a few feet and was into the water of the King tides. It was a long wade to the well; I had never dreamt the distance was so far. A huge green crab scuttled from the water-logged grasses, his great nippers raised menacingly as he backed away. When near the well I saw on the mangrove branches above it a little crowd of birds closely huddled together, wings limply outstretched, beaks open, gasping under the brazen sun. One glance was sufficient. The tide had overflowed the well.

1 1

Thirst

We lay all day in the tent. To have wandered about in that stifling heat would have developed thirst unbearable. Gloomy thoughts those, while lying there staring at the tent roof. Under this catastrophe Charlie must succumb to the spell of one of his most morose moods.

"What shall we do?" I ventured.

"Put up with it until the tides go down of course," he growled.

"How long will that be?"

"Four or five days, a week perhaps." "We'll be dead by that time!"

"What odds?"

"If you wish to leave your bones on this desolate patch, I don't. Let us do something, even if we only dig at the foot of the Peak. We might find water, a soakage spring from the hill or something."

"Find hell! Long before we found it we'd be raving mad with thirst. Digging without water, looking for water in this heat!"

"How do the birds find water then? They've lived all their lives on the island and must have seen numbers of King tides come and go. They must have some place to drink."

"They have. The well. Otherwise they wouldn't be panting their hearts out there now. They're acclimatized and do the same as we must do—wait until the tides go down and don't flutter a feather while they're doing it either."

"Perhaps they get dew on the grass," I suggested.

"Dew on my eye!" . . . Charlie glowered up at the tent pole during the remainder of the day—a fearfully long day. It seemed that the sun was never going to set.

Lying there that night with open mouth, almost panting from thirst, I heard a quickly silenced groan. Presently in the silence I heard Charlie gasping.

"What is the matter, old man? Are you in pain?"

He grunted.

"What if I put a billy of sea water on and make you a hot flannel or something? Anything I can do I'm only too willing."

He did not answer immediately. Then with half-sunken eyes staring from ghastly face he glared over his shoulder.

"You can go to hell. If I'm keeping you awake, get out of the tent." And he rolled over on his side.

The following day dragged by breathlessly. We could not eat. That night was maddening. We lay there breathing heavily, the air so dull that the smoke was a misty vapour with barely strength to rise to the top of the tent. From outside, the angry hum of insects irritated already badly frayed nerves.

Next morning I walked down to the well. The water gleaming around it mocked one. But the tides were receding. To-night, if we bailed the water out and bailed again in the morning we might win a brackish drink. We might! We would both go mad soon if we did not; our tongues were thickening already. A little bird lay half in the water, half on a mangrove root. Perhaps it had drunk of the water, or it may have fallen dead from the branch above where its mates crouched helplessly. A big green crab was reaching up from the roots; there was something evil in the way its bulk came slithering up from the water, one huge claw reaching over the root for the bird. I waded across to the little dead thing and tossed it back on to the grass. But the grass was under water and it sank down. Dully I waded back to it, thinking to carry it right back to camp to dry ground where the crabs would not get it.

Away outside the mangroves, the reef was eight feet under water, so transparent that it looked only to be inches deep, so still that it was apparently frozen. Then a big fish, moving effortlessly, his eyes like polished glass, glided by. I began slowly climbing the Peak. The grass was drooping; the granite rocks gave forth an awful heat. From the summit was visible a steamer gliding swiftly north. I waved my arms and yelled while searching frenziedly for a match, then rushed down the Peak to the camp. Seizing a firestick I panted "Steamer" to Charlie, then tackled the Peak, lighting the grass as I panted on, to crawl gasping to the summit.

But the steamer grew swiftly smaller like a living thing skimming over glass. Something came panting behind me and there was Charlie, his red-rimmed eyes all blinking from the smoke, his lips swollen and cracking, his mouth open like the beaks of the birds on the tree by the well. He stood and stared without looking at me. Then:

"It's no good," he croaked. "We might be niggers for all they know."

"They've got glasses!"

"Yes. So had Nelson. If we don't get a drink to-morrow night at the latest* we're done."

"The water will have gone back past the well to-night—we can bail it out!"

"Yes. So long as the salt water has not penetrated too deep into the spring, we'll be all right."

We sat there a while, gazing at sea flashing under the sun. A column of smoke from the burnt grass clouded up over the Peak. Charlie stood up, coughing, and slouched away, hardly casting any shadow. I followed, feeling there was no oil in my joints. A burning thirst suddenly urged me to start shouting and curse the sea.

At sundown we bailed out the well and dug down into the muddy sand. The water that so slowly welled up was salty. We crouched there then and presently bailed it out again, keeping on until the sand-flies drove us maddened, back to the tent. That was an awful night. At daylight, without a word, we hobbled down to the well. It was full—and salty. We bailed it out and crawled back to the shelter of the tent. I did not want to die of thirst—not in the heat; it would be too terrible.

Near midday we crawled down to the well again—the little birds were sitting around the stones, their feathers and wings all puffed out, they were chirping now and again. I ran as fast as I could, Charlie hobbling after. We bent down our heads like animals. Thank God, the water was drinkable, though salty. We lay there quite a while, lowering our faces now and again to the nostrils in water.

This narrow escape from an awful death made us good cobbers again— but only for a couple of days. The privation had made Charlie's "gas" accumulate. He was suffering terribly, but refused the relief even of sympathy. There was nothing at all that I could do for him. The King tides had rapidly receded to normal; so we turned to our fishing, each to his own side of the island. One day, gloomily, I made back to the camp. Life was pretty rough, nothing but thirst and sand-flies, nothing to smoke, only fish and crabs to eat. The hardest thing of all was not to be able to laugh.

With a joke now and then life would be bearable, even interesting, until the ketch came. The ketch! There was no chance of the ketch until this awful calm broke. Throwing down the fish by the fire, I picked up a billy can, turned for the well, and met Charlie with two billies brimming full. Taking a pannikin, I filled and raised it when it was knocked from my lips and Charlie's blazing eyes were glaring into mine.

"Get your own water," he hissed. "Think I carry water for you? Curse you!" I dodged his furious blow.

"You crazy fool!" I snarled. "If you come at me I'll finish you. And I don't want to swing for a swine like you."

"Hit me where you like if you can and be damned to you," he screamed. I thought he was going to fly at me, but a glimmering of intelligence held him, trembling violently. I turned abruptly and walked swiftly away, up the Peak.

Here was an awful thing. Two men on an island; one half crazy, the other feeling himself almost going so. A terrible thought. If we had actually fought there was no knowing what might have happened. No one was there to stop us. We should have gone mad, fought like wild beasts. Those eyes of his, that mouth amidst a stubble of beard, brought vivid memory of a hospital ship in the war days when a poor crazed patient escaped from the detention ward, ran the length of the ship and with mad cries leapt overboard. What if we did eventually come to blows and Charlie got the better of me! In self-preservation it would mean only one blow upon that dreadful wound of his. Charlie's face and crouch had shown that he realized this.

There was not a sail, not a smoke drift in sight. Thirstily, I walked down the Peak to the well. What if Charlie was really going mad! Mad men were said to be very cunning . . . Wouldn't it be best quietly to take the bolt out of his pea rifle? . . . What if he hit me on the head with a tomahawk while I was asleep!

A soft breath of wind kissed my cheek. I stopped, then stared—fairly ran back up the Peak. Far out to sea was a tiny vapour like a trill of foam that vanished. The green and level sea was intensely still. Again that breath fanned my face, this time a moment longer, a divine coolness. It came again, and the face of the sea broke into wrinkles. They spread and spread, grew wider and bigger and larger until, with a sparkling foam on their caps, they came racing towards the island. Gone was the glassy sea, reborn into restless moving life. The ripples had now grown into foam-flecked waves which slowly rolled as they came loping on in ever-increasing volume.

I laughed hysterically and raced down to tell Charlie. He was standing outside the camp watching the wind rippling the grasses. "Good-bye to the sand-flies!" I yelled.

"Yes," he growled. "They're finished." "How soon will the ketch come now?"

"She ought to be along in a week with this breeze working up."

We climbed the Peak and stood in the wind watching the sea rolling. Then gazed back out over the green of the mangrove forest. The great canopy was all astir, rippling sunlight trembled from a billion rustling leaves. There came to us a whispering, an eerie moan. From the little scrubby patch on the Peak side near us birds were spreading tremulous wings in swift flight down to the well and back again, whistling and chirping. We climbed to the very top of the Peak. A strong wind whistled through the grasses that now were swaying and bowing like living things in happy dance. Overhead, clouds were flying across the sky. A heavy sea rolled in big breakers upon the reef. The world of noise and movement and life had come back to us again.

"I'm as hungry as a horse," I laughed. "The tide is out; I'm going fishing. How about it?"

"Yes," he growled cordially. We hurried down to camp for the spears.

1 2

The Wind

That night, in ecstasy we lay awake drinking in a joyous chorus. One great swelling song rose from the mangrove forest with a shrill trilling from the countless leaves in between gusts of wind.

From the outside reef a thunderous roar grew hourly, especially when the tide came rolling in. Then from over the reef came broken combers to surge in little waves across the lagoon and splash on the tiny beach within a few yards of the tent. The tent door was wide open; gone were all the sand-flies, blown far out to sea we fervently hoped. All was coolness and sound and sweet wind. We lay smoking, for Charlie had actually offered me some of his tobacco, dried seaweed. I had tried to smoke dried mangrove leaves and grass, and as cigars, different varieties of porous roots. All poisonous stuff. But Charlie was obstinate enough to force himself to do something he disliked, just to accustom himself to it; he made himself eat bits of shark and the flippers of stingray when sweeter fish were easy to hand.

That night was a heaven-sent relief, mentally as well as physically. We yarned on the friendliest terms far into the night; fervently I hoped we would remain so. And through it all was the knowledge that now the wind had come the ketch must come too.

Next morning at daylight we rolled from bunk and stepped out on to the beach. A howling wind nearly carried us off our feet. Some of the lagoon mangroves were uprooted and were the sport of mad waves that swirled right in over the reef to toss their spray high among the. torn branches now writhing above the beach. The coral sand was carpeted thickly with leaves, and the reef was blanketed in far- flung masses of foam. It was glorious.

"By Jove! won't the old ketch just bounce along in this breeze!"

Charlie, without replying, watched a cloud of white-breasted storm-birds passing overhead, wind-driven at terrific speed.

"I hope it's not going to blow a gale. The ketch might not be able to sail at all."

Charlie nodded out towards the reef.

"Even if they were fools enough to leave shelter, how do you think a boat is going to land in that?" The cauldron on the reef thundered the answer. My heart sank.

When the tide surged out we hurried to our fishing. The coolness and relief had made us famishing. Birds were singing around the well.

To be able to walk about bare-armed and bare-legged, our faces no longer plastered in mud, was heavenly. In holiday spirit we ventured into what was the unknown to me, Charlie's fishing-ground. Mine was behind the Peak, his on the other side of the Hill. There the waters, coming in over the reef to the lagoon swept on into the mangroves, but were very shallow at low tide. This inlet from the lagoon was river wide, walled by the mangrove forest to the east and a thin wall of trees to the west. Along the sea edge of these trees the ocean was roaring on a huge esplanade of the reef unknown to me. We waded up the shallow inlet upon its white sandy bottom, clean and pleasant and open to the sky after the gloomy mud creeks of the inner mangroves. Russet brown sea-grass rubbed broad leaves against our legs, so that we trod warily lest some big crab or nee-dle-toothed eel try a bite at our toes. To right and left, here and there, little creeks branched off into the mangroves, their gloomy recesses intriguing with the probability of big fish lurking among the mangrove roots.

Presently we came to a broad cross-channel that spread out from the mangrove forest to run into the opposite mangroves and, apparently, through them and over the great reef into the sea. This channel, under seagrass, was like a lucerne patch. We yelled and plunged forward simultaneously—too late, for the turtle sped past our very legs in a twisting dodge, his long, snake-like head outstretched, his flippers working at top speed. Dodging our spears he fairly skimmed over the grass tops, his broad carapace just cleaving the surface. In keenest disappointment we watched his escape. How beautifully juicy a steak from him would have tasted.

"I wish we could find a nest. Turtle eggs would be a treat."

"No hope," answered Charlie. "This island is all coral; the turtles like to lay in sandy beaches. Only a stray comes here."

"We might get a dugong."

"No chance. We'd need a harpoon if we saw one."

"I wonder what they ate for breakfast in Cooktown this morning."

"Fried eggs, most likely, with bacon and potato chips. Bread and butter and coffee, toast for them as like it and a row with the missus as like as not . . . This is a likely looking creek for fish." Charlie waded towards an opening in the mangroves. We speared our fish in the little side creeks where fish were plentiful, all nice and cosy in the still pools so sheltered from the now raging storm outside. It came to us as gusts of wind with a distinctly increasing roar from the surf. We waded along and picked the fish out as they lay pressed against the roots —just one quick jab with the spear. We seldom missed. Our eyes were rapidly growing accustomed to the deceptiveness of the water and the merging of the fish's skin with the bark root against which he was sheltering.

"We've got plenty now," said Charlie as he hung a wriggling butter-fish on his belt. "What if we have a stroll along the reef before the tide comes in."

As we pushed through the outer mangrove fringe the wind fairly took our breath away. The tops of the trees there were being lashed down on to the coral. Easy to understand now why Nature in this extremely shallow soil had strengthened their grip by giving them so many roots. Their dwarfed trunks with tough, thin limbs, grew small tough leaves that offered little wind resistance. They had to be tough trees to survive; and they were tough, defying both wind and sea. Now we had to shout to be heard above the thunder on the reef. As far as the eye could see the broad reef was one tumbling lather of foam, magnificent in sight and sound. We walked along it for half a mile, like walking upon the far-flung battlements of some mighty wall. Which it was, withstanding the siege of the sea for unnumbered centuries. Its surface was honeycombed with grottoed pools that would be a wonder to examine on some calm day. Sticking up from the coral, rusted and overgrown with weeds, we came on the woebegone fragment of a ship. The sea is cruel. Looking back, we could see above the trees the tops of the two little hills. They looked a surprisingly long way off. We hurried back, but before we reached the lagoon channel a wind-driven tide was lashing at our knees.

That afternoon the wind had increased to a howling gale. And for the next fortnight, without cessation, the island shores were walls of flying foam, even the shrieking wind half- drowned in the pounding thunder. Clouds raced overhead. To climb up to the Peak was almost impossible, a man would have been bowled over and over and rolled down into the sea. The long grasses were pressed flat to the Peak's sides; the little birds rarely ventured from the scrubby patch on the sheltered side of the Peak. When they sped down for water they flew low, skimming the ground; and they skimmed the grass in flying back again.

The days dragged wearily by. One night while lying awake listening for a diminution in the roar of the breakers, we heard a piercing scream right over the tent, distinctly followed by the beat of powerful wings. What mad night bird was out in all that fury is hard to say. Its despairing screech almost froze my blood. I couldn't sleep—felt itchy all over, uneasy, and gnawingly hungry. If only we had some dripping or fat we could fry fish for a change and use the fat on damper as butter. I wished Charlie would say something; he was restless, too, tossing and grunting. He had grown moody again these last few days, prowling away to his own fishing grounds until I took the hint and went back to the mangrove forest. I hesitated to force conversation lest he flare up or lapse deeper into the sulks.

Slowly the night wore on. Ears grow acutely keen in such circumstances. Charlie was not restless through pain alone.

"It's an irritable sort of night," I ventured. "Can't you sleep?"

"Gr-r!" he snarled, and slinging off his blanket jumped up and took it to the galley fire. In the light of the wind-blown blaze he knelt down and studiously examined the blanket. A wild looking chap, kneeling there with his hair all over his eyes and his shirt blown up over his shoulders. I wondered what had bitten him now. Suddenly he howled and flinging the blanket aside rushed into the tent, seized his clothes, and raced to the beach. He slung all his things into the little tumbling waves coming in from the lagoon. Whipping off his shirt, he followed them, bursting into a torrent of hysterical cursing.

I was too startled to realize instantly what had happened. Then it dawned on me that there must be insects of some description in the blankets. Of course! It was an overwhelming relief. For a moment it seemed that Charlie was a lunatic. I laughed and chuckled for quite a time, then collected the blanket and the few rags and took them to a tree near the galley, shook the blanket in the wind, then turned in under a tree. I didn't envy Charlie standing out there in the dark, cold water with broken branches sliding against his legs, not to mention clumsy seaweed and coral and stuff.

Suddenly he dashed back to the tent; in a trice he had it and the fly unrigged and flung into the water; threw all our things out into the dark, then made a bonfire on the spot where the tent had been. I watched in growing anger. It would have been laughable had we not been just two men quite alone. I tried to distinguish whether it was temper or something more serious that had so upset him.

Suddenly he realized that the waves were tossing his clothes all over the beach. With a yell he chased them, a wild, brown figure in the light of the wind-blown bonfire. Vindictively, I almost felt sorry that the sandflies had gone.

13

The Well

When at long last that fortnight of storm blew itself out, Charlie was not feeling in companion-able mood. So, except when fishing or sleeping, I climbed to the Lookout away up on the Peak. There, for me, while staring all around out over the sea and away towards the mainland, the daylight hours passed on leaden feet. Several *beche-de-mer* luggers were one day visible far out towards the Great Barrier Reef, their sails, no larger than handkerchiefs, glinting like the sun-kissed wings of sea birds. But not a sign of the ketch.

One morning I was sitting moodily by the galley fire when Charlie unexpectedly asked. "Where did you buy your rug in Cooktown?" "From Billy Jackson."

"That's where the bugs came from! You brought them here!"

In amazement I stared at the threatening face.

"Nonsense. Billy wouldn't sell me a blanket from his own home with bugs in it!—But if he did, what odds?"

"This was a clean island; any man could have settled here in peace. And now, you civilized beast, you've brought bugs to it!"

He struck me on the face. I jumped up and we got into it, hammer and tongs. We clinched and went down, struggling madly as we rolled over the galley fire striking and kicking and wrenching. I struck him on the temple and his grip eased; and loosened altogether to fierce thumps below the ribs. He rolled off gasping, then leapt up and in long staggering bounds made for the tent. His face warned me that momentarily he had gone quite mad.

I ran straight for the mangroves down by the well and plunged in amongst the sheltering trunks as a bullet whistled past, then another struck a dappled trunk with a vicious thud. But I was safe, running swiftly on, plunging through the mud and leaping from root to root with a surety and speed apparently impossible. Thank heaven the tide was still out. The farthest place from that madman's rifle was the granite mound.

Ten minutes later I was through the mangroves and climbing up amongst the massed granite boulders. Here was abundance of cover; with ordinary caution a man would be quite safe from a lurking shot from the mangroves. Somehow I did not expect that shot, Charlie by now might be sorry the whole thing had happened. I hoped fervently he was. His weapon was only a short range pea rifle, but it was a rifle for all that. What an idiot I'd been not to steal the bolt, when I had known for some time past how events might turn. From the summit of the Mound I crouched, searching back over the mangrove tops towards the Peak and the Hill. But I saw no living thing. A thousand yards distant, the Peak and the Hill rose abruptly above the mass of heavy green mangrove foliage, with blue of sky above and green of sea around.

The only time that madman could reach the Mound would be when the tide was out. Then the great encircling reef and the mangrove forest would be bare of water except for pools in the creeks. And then if he came along the great broad reef he would be plainly visible. Not so if he came through the mangroves which grew right to the Mound. The tide was now coming swirling in over the reef and racing into the mouths of the creeks, spreading out with each oncoming wave to sweep among the mangrove roots with loud, sucking gurgles. Soon it would rise up over the roots and begin to suck at the trunks themselves. Not even a madman could cross them. Besides, dorsal fins appeared suddenly, racing up the deepening creeks and disappearing into the mangroves. Here was safety for the coming twelve hours anyway.

I sat back and thought things out. Two fools of men on a barren island, and they could not live together for a miserable few months. How tragically absurd. Our very lives, apparently, depended on our helping one another. This was no well-watered tropical island rich with fruits and vegetables and game: here human life must fight hard for survival. Surely to goodness we should have made an effort, and another and another effort, to be friends. For some time past it had been perfectly obvious, too, that even when the ketch did appear she would not be able to land a boat except under most favourable conditions. Yet, here were two lunatics at one another's throats.

I blamed myself a lot. Charlie was not altogether responsible; he must suffer hell whenever that "gas" accumulated in his stomach. But how was I to know that the man was a walking chemist's shop, and that life to him was supposed to depend on daily medical treatment? It was not my fault that he had been drunk and left his instrument and chemicals behind in Cooktown. But when all was said and done, I was the lucky man. I had youth and perfect health. I did not bear a grudge against the world, but looked on it as a wonderful playground with this island but an episode. All life was an adventure, and I had hardly started on it. It was foolish to become downhearted now. Even here I knew how to get my own tucker; impossible to starve. It only meant living and waiting until the ketch should come.

Heavens! The fish spear! It was back at the camp. Fire? Thankfully I remembered I could make fire; I'd watched the natives do it often enough; merely the patient rubbing together of two dry sticks until a wee-puff of flame should light the grassy tinder. Water? That was a terrible thought. The well was on Charlie's side of the island. What if his madness lasted for some days! He might wait at the well, hidden in the mangroves. It would mean only a few days at most. I had shot dingoes that way; waited in ambush at the station tank for them to come and drink.

How about venturing across to drink at night? Impossible. Even on nights when the tide was out hardly any man could get safely through those eerie mangroves with their million entangling roots, the million overhead branches sheltering blackness that held acres of treacherous mud; waterholes harbouring giant sea eels with the teeth of devils; stranded giant cods and sharks in the inlet pools; worse still, the unknown terrors that come with the night. The possibility of a stray crocodile, too. Vividly I remembered, when we were sailing past the Turtle Group, seeing a crocodile swimming far out to sea. And I had shot crocodiles away opposite on the coast, at Cape Melville. No, I would suffer much before chancing those mangroves at night. Besides, Charlie could wait by the well at night just the same, even better.

Relief came with the thought that Charlie's madness was only temporary. Almost certainly he would now be lying out in the lagoon on the flat rock pouring sea-water into that tube, sorry in his own way that the whole thing had happened. We were two lonely men, and now in a nasty position. Completely isolated, we were existing, lucky that we could exist, on a barren island. There was only one little water supply. Still, we could both keep alive while not active enemies. But if one were to attempt to hold the water against the other, there could be only one outcome — the survival of the fitter.

In an uneasy medley of thoughts, I passed a miserable afternoon; the sunset was lonely. I searched for a hiding-place, some deep, walled-in crevice. Animals search that way. I found a place, down through a narrow cleft where, ten feet below, the black darkness widened out into a rough chamber. The roof of this gloomy little cavern was a mass of boulders wedged one against another. Grim and cold and foreboding it looked and felt, the dying rays of the sun filtering half way down the crevice. But it promised safety from surprise.

After sunset I put in time carrying dry sand in a big shell up from the reef and dropping it down the crevice. A man must have something to lie on; the stone down below was hard, and already cold. I would have given my kingdom for a match.

That night was devilish lonely. A light sea breeze played all manner of queer noises among the rocks, half-heard whistlings and sighs, and faint whisperings. During a momentary lull a foraging crab slithered over a rock somewhere outside, like sand-paper scraping over pebbles. Ever and again sounded a furious splashing as big fish fought in the flooded creek nearby. Robinson Crusoe was very lucky. The company of a good black-fellow here would have been welcome indeed.

But the water problem meant life or death. How could I get that water?

At the first sheen of dawn I was up on top of the Mound, staring towards the Peak and the Hill growing plainer every moment. There was no sign of life. Yesterday and last night seemed a nightmare. With the sun came cheeriness. Almost certainly Charlie would have recovered his sanity; everything would be all right. I grinned a bit, thinking of the stupid foolishness of yesterday, and wished the tide was out so that I could hurry straight back along the reef and walk into camp and say "Good day!" But there came a sinking feeling at memory of Charlie's bad spells. They lasted more than one day. Out at sea, not a sail dipped in all that expanse of lazily tumbling waters. What on earth had happened to the ketch? Surely she had not gone down in that last spell of bad weather? If so, a boat would have put out from Cooktown to look for her and for us too—unless the authorities thought the ketch had picked us up and we had all gone down together.

Water! And something to hold the water in! What an awful lot of things a man really needed, just to live.

There were three billy cans and a kerosene tin bucket at the tent. But Charlie had possession there. There were any amount of big bucket-like shells on the reef though; they would hold water—once I got it. Longingly I thought of that spear, and of a firestick. Yes, and a blanket and shaving gear, for I'd suddenly seen my whiskered face and tangled hair reflected from a pool. I did not want to become like Charlie, even in looks.

The tide was just on the turn. What if I tried to get through the mangroves while the tide was still running out! He would not expect me at the well until the tide was right out. If I got there before he expected me. ... A sudden thought! Nothing to carry water in; no spear; no fire. If I could make sure Charlie was waiting at the well, I could creep back to the reef, then, sheltered by the mangroves, run along the sea edge to the Peak, run around down beside the lagoon to the tiny beach, and so to the tent. If he was not waiting at the well it would mean he was quite all right. I'd simply walk on up to the camp and we'd make it up and carry on as before. But more pleasantly.

I laughed at the tide now rushing out. Everything was solved; all was well and life a joke after all. It really does take a lot to kill a man.

When I entered the mangroves the water was still two feet above the roots, swirling its gurgling way back to sea with the violence of a mountain torrent. The real joy of solving a problem that had looked impossible temporarily banished thirst and hunger, while the active job ahead banished all thoughts of fear. It was a tough task half wading, half swimming the first big creek—the worst. Then came the mangroves and the need to keep a foothold on the bow-like roots under water. Almost instinctively I now knew those treacherous portions of a root that would collapse underfoot; but under the running water sometimes a root would be difficult to distinguish, and down I'd slip clawing into the maze. The outlets to the sea were the worst, only a few yards across, but wild with swirling water. It was a case of leaping in, chancing sharks, and struggling across while whirled downstream until the twisted roots opposite were close enough to grip. An apparently impossible job made possible and comparatively easy only by experience gained in fishing daily among the mangroves.

I came out into open sunlight on the reef side nearly at the foot of the Peak. The well was three hundred yards sharp to the left, just within the mangrove edge. A few triumphant breaths, then, taking a risk, I ran along the firm coral-strewn ground until within a hundred yards of the well, ducked in among the mangroves, and advanced stealthily. Surely Charlie could not expect me yet if he really was going to wait for me at all. Then I saw the stonework of the well, and thirst came at once, aggravated perhaps by the plunges through salt water. There was no sign of Charlie. But he could be hidden anywhere amongst the tangled maze of roots and branches and trunks surrounding the well. The silence was unearthly except for the twittering. ...

I almost laughed. A dozen yellow-breasted birds were hopping on the stone-work of the well engaged in a lazy conversational chirrup, while prettily indulging in a fluttering bath in the shallow water. Those tiny splashes sounded liquid sweet.

As I stepped forward to drink, the birds flew to the mangrove tops squawking indignantly —and Charlie appeared. I crouched amongst the roots. He bent over the stone-work and drank long and deep, remaining a few minutes to gaze reflectively into the water as the drops fell from his grizzled beard. Then, bending down, he carefully examined the mud all around the well. This deliberate searching for tracks banished all feelings of the peace I had hoped for between us.

Apparently satisfied, he leisurely climbed a gnarled mangrove whose leafy branches spread directly over the well. The birds, in noisy indignation at this sacrilege to their private domain, flew in all directions.

14

A Man Must Drink

I slipped back through the mangroves, emerged at the reef and started at a run around the shore edge of the Peak, jumping from boulder to boulder. It was to be war then, Charlie was out to get me and I was out to live. Once around the Peak I was soon on the front shore of the reef again, skirting the lagoon. The tiny beach looked strangely familiar. And there stood the tent.

Everything was the same. The tent door shut, the fire carefully banked up, the kerosene tin and three billies full of crystal-clear water. Eagerly I drank.

Since the perish during the King tides we had always kept the billies full of water. With delight I found the spear; the feel of it on the hand brought surprising confidence. It was the work of a' moment to seize the blankets and make a swag of the few personal belongings, then grasp a firestick and fan it into flame. I passed the spear haft through the handles of two full billy cans, seized the handle of the kerosene tin bucket, and started back the way I had come.

When near the lagoon edge just about to round the Peak and well away from the camp, I paused for a breather, and noticed something half buried in the shingle above high tide. It proved to be the log of the *Sea Foam*, the old Malay's cutter. Very much the worse for wear; still it was readable, though most of it was in Malay. There were many empty leaves. It gave one a queer feeling to open the salted pages of this sea-wrecked relic and read it again, even though the contents were but the short words of the sea, or accounts of the sale of *beche-de-mer*, or orders on Chinese storekeepers for provisions. Eagerly I added this battered old sea log to the load; it would be something to read to-night. Then I hurried along, pausing now and then to whirl the firestick and keep it well alight.

Charlie would be very angry at the loss of the billy cans. But he would not need them; he had the whole well all to himself. Oddly enough, they were my own billy cans; I had bought them in Cooktown and as an after-thought brought along the kerosene tin bucket as well.

It was a hefty load, but the water was far more valuable than gold. The tide was now draining out, and it was possible to wade easily along the reef, though with many a backward glance. Thankfully I reached the Mound.

It is wonderful how adversity and the chance of more to come make a man think. Charlie would certainly visit me; if not almost immediately, on some future day when he was again in the grip of his trouble. If he came while I was in the mangroves fishing he would find the water. He mustn't find the water.

Craftily I found a hiding-place down towards the sea edge but above reach of the highest tide; a crevice in which the kerosene tin and billies fitted as if the place had been chiselled out for them. And nearby a long, flat stone like a board to cover the top. Sprinkled with sand, it looked perfectly natural. All around it was bare rock, so there was no chance of leaving a betraying track.

Hurriedly throwing drift-wood down into the cavern home I climbed down and started a fire, rolling on logs that could not possibly burn out. Then seizing the spear, I climbed up to the open sunlight, glanced back once along the reef, lovingly balanced the spear, and dived into the man-groves, hungry and eager as any hunter. With an easy mind, too, indepen-dent now of everything.

The tide was well out; the fishing excellent —and enhanced by the interest of "exploratory" work. For I avoided my usual haunts and pressed farther into the mangroves, locating several new creeks. The -pools in this part of the island were different; the fish had to be detected in their varying hiding- places; new mud holes had to be tested be-fore a man dare plunge across them. Finding new creeks was going to bring new interest in the days to come. And there might be adventure any day; in these lab-yrinths of shallow water and roots, I might come on a big old dugong left by the tide. Visions of a fat old sea cow brought a hungry gloating for fresh meat. The sea cow's plenteous steaks taste much like bacon; and a sea cow with calf would hold at least a kerosene tin full of milk.

A few hours later and I was back on top of the Mound picking the bones of two big cod, glancing every now and then back along the reef towards the Peak. The last glance became an apprehensive gaze. A thousand yards away by the foot of the Peak, and coming along the reef, was Charlie. I tried to detect whether he was still in mad mood or coming to make it

He approached rapidly and waved threatening arms. He wanted those billy cans and everything else I'd taken.

I clambered down the Mound and quickly carried up armfuls of decent-sized stones. This was my castle and it now had to stand a siege. Charlie could remain within attacking distance only until the tide began to come in; he would be forced to retreat then. If I avoided him by slipping into the mangroves, then he could raid the camp; could do so repeatedly and enjoy himself. No, he must keep to his side of the island and I would keep to mine, with the tides between us. If he decided otherwise, then he would learn that even with his pop-gun he would not have much chance at a wary man amongst these boulders.

Charlie, reaching the bottom of the Mound, began to climb the boul-ders. In ambush I waited until I could see his glaring eyes, then let him have a barrage.

He ducked and slipped, clutching as he rolled. A stone smashed into fragments beside his head, splathering his face with splinters. He must have been badly shaken, for he scrambled up and leapt back from boulder to boulder followed by whizzing stones. When he gained the reef he ran like something really mad. It was an unexpectedly easy victory. Time was to prove that when Charlie took these bad turns a shock would jerk him back to normal.

Lonely days went by. There was no sign of Charlie though he surely must have recovered by now. It was impossible to see him unless he climbed the Peak or came down my side of the reef. He rarely did either. To-morrow when low tide came I decided to walk along the reef and erect a flag of distress up-on the Lookout, and from there peep down on Charlie's camp. I had the depressing feeling that after one of his turns he might die, and I did not want the poor devil to die alone. That, I was to learn, was the very thing he wished to do.

The sun was great company. With the dying of night faint glows of light would seep down through the crevices and the boulders would gradually take ghostly shape; one slender pillar was my "Lady in Grey." When gathering light proved her to be only stone, I would arise. Over the sea the sun would pop up, a glowing ball of red and gold balanced as if upon a hair line. The two unfriendly men folk, the land birds and the sea birds all brightened up with the coming of the sun. No doubt many species of the fish and crabs did too. With an occasional harsh croak, the grey and blue and white cranes would come down from their mangrove perches to alight by the mud holes. In stately fashion they would presently begin fishing for breakfast.

The landward side of the Mound grew perhaps a hundred of the same hardy, dwarfed trees that clung to the sheltered side of the Peak. And among these lived a few of the little yellowish-green birds whose comrades lived on the Peak and the Hill. With a lively twittering after sunrise, my birds would fly over the mangrove forest to the well. There they would drink and bathe and enjoy an hour's gossip with their comrades. Then they would return to the Mound and go about their daily business. If it happened to be a hot midday they would fly again to the well and indulge in a bath and chat with their cobbers. But if the day was cool this second visit was made towards sunset for the evening drink and chatter.

A few other birds kept to the gloom of the mangrove forest. These were seldom seen; they were very quiet and had the knack of disappearing like fleeting shadows. They reminded me of the fish that could stare within a foot of a man, but be invisible to him. In the mangroves a man might suddenly, though only balf-consciously, come eye to eye with such a bird; but in a second it would have disappeared behind a leaf.

Sitting up on top of the Mound I used to watch, and be watched by, a colony of old and young cranes fishing around a large mud pool down at the base of the Mound. It was on the landward side just over the reef, a wide shimmering pool as large as a couple of tennis- courts, surrounded by mangroves. It had surprised me to find cranes on the island; but exploring trips into the heart of the mangroves revealed hidden pools and much wider creeks each of which homed its cranes—quiet, solemn, wide-awake birds that shrewdly watched the approach of the strange man-animal while warily refusing to be flurried. I got to know every one of the cranes in the pool below me, the quaint actions of the long-legged bodies and solemn, knowing heads, the hoarse peculiarity of each raucous voice. There was a white old patriarch with a bent bill and leery eye, a wise old chap with a quaint habit of turning his head sideways, as if saying: "Now watch *me*, young one, and I'll teach you something." Always close beside this old fellow was a lively little blue crane with a hoppy leg. Most likely when a baby his leg had been snapped at by a big fish, or a more awful eel. Among them all was the most solemn crane imaginable—a deep thinker. He would suddenly startle his companions by a series of hoarse calls. And they would energetically applaud in chorus. Idly I wondered why the birds never fished in the centre of this pool but always walked carefully around the outer edge. Perhaps the mud in the centre was too treacherously sticky even to support the weight of a crane.

Next day at low tide I walked along the reef skirting the mangroves to the Peak; climbed it, and from the top looked down at Charlie's camp. There was no sign of him; he was away fishing doubtless.

The Peak was a far better lookout than the Mound; it rose almost two hundred feet straight up from the sea. From this height one could look upon a wide sweep of sparkling ocean; but there was no sign of sail or smoke. The mainland fifteen miles away was visible now as a smudgy haze. How I longed to be on that mainland. No bird was caged more securely than we were.

Charlie emerged from the lagoon mangroves. He was staring up as he walked across the open towards his camp. He bent over his banked- up fire. I longed to go down and make it up. But he might not have fully recovered; perhaps it would be wiser to wait a few days. It would be wise, too, to fill the water buckets tomorrow, and keep them always full in between Charlie's bad turns.

I hurried back to the Mound intent on getting in my fishing before the tide turned. The tide regulated everything. Impossible to fish in the mangroves while the tide was in, and without lines one could not fish in the sea. When the tide was out we could prowl all over the island, always remembering that we must hurry back when the tide turned. With the tide in, we were completely marooned to the Peak or Hill or Mound. Next day I filled the kerosene tin' bucket and billy cans, but saw no sign of Charlie. Several days later I waited near his camp, but he didn't appear. Almost certainly he was watching from the mangroves, for I waited until the tide began coming in before hurrying back to the Mound.

The greatest weariness of this island was its tiny size, apart from the mangrove forest. If a man could only have gone for long walks it would have helped to pass time away. But when the tide was in he was marooned on the few acres of land around the Peak and the Hill— as though he were sitting on a log upon the wide sea.

Another fortnight passed and peculiar weather came. The shadowy mainland was blotted out by storm clouds that travelled swiftly to engulf the island as billowing clouds of mist shutting out sea and sky and islands. Twenty minutes later they would be swiftly blown away, and brilliant sunshine would momentarily show the mainland with miles of sparkling waves in between. Then clouds and mist would quickly gather again and enfold all. Southward it was somewhat clearer, the big bulk of Lizard Island standing up sheer and bold from a savage sea. Lizard Island was about fifteen miles away. Often I wished that Fate had landed us there instead of on this tiny speck. But there was no mangrove forest there, so we should not have had the fish and crabs to live upon. It came as a shock to realize that this forlorn hole had its compensations. On that much larger island we might have perished.

Lizard Island, like so many others along the lonely peninsula coast, had known its tragedy. Mrs Watson with her baby and the wounded Chinaman were driven from it by the blacks, who, waiting until the men folk sailed away, canoed across from the distant mainland to attack them. In the dead of night the woman, baby, and Chinaman crawled down to the beach from the hut, then, inch by inch, launched the half of a sawn-off iron tank, and drifted away in it with the tide. It was a time of dead calm and blazing days. They drifted to this very island. The Chinaman crawled ashore right where Charlie's camp was now, crawled right around the Peak seeking water. The tragedy of it, that there should be water within easy reach—but hidden in the mangroves and the mud. Naturally the Chinaman crawled back, shaking his head. Again they drifted for suffocating days in the iron tub, then stranded on the barren Turtle Group. The Chinaman was a gentleman; he crawled away because he did not want the "Missy" to see him die. She wrote in her diary until the last. Mist wreaths now blotted Lizard Island from view, and great black clouds came rushing from the mainland.

Surely this weather would bring rain!

15

She Sailed Away

Those nights were lonely! The old fire, throwing into bright relief the boulders round about, was company. I sat and stared into it for hours. And it used to trace such dancing patterns and pictures upon the boulders. One could conjure up any scene so long as the flames were not too bright to throw those flickering shadows. With a little cheery fire enlivened by draughts stealing through the crevices, Roman armies and Pharaoh's spearmen and camel trains and prehistoric things would march and glide across the boulders, and fade away into caverns.

Fire must have been the prehistoric man's great friend, as it is the aboriginal's companion and helpmate to-day. In its friendship at night he draws comfort and dreams things when alone, and, in company, plans things and gives his thoughts to others; and so grim night slips by unnoticed. With it he smokes out his game, cooks his food, hardens his weapons, and burns out logs to make canoes.

Not all the nights on the Mound were silent. The surf breaking against the reef at the foot of the Mound was deep rolling thunder until the tide came flooding in and cushioned the reef. I could picture that tide always from the sound, could see it rising inch by inch. The clear reef breaking the waves in murmuring thunder. The growing harshness as the world tipped slightly over and more water came rolling towards the reef. The deepening thunder as the world tipped farther and still more water came rolling in. The angry boom as the reef tried its hardest to hold back the irresistible flow. Then the triumphant roar as the. first massed waves broke right upon the reef and came, broken and slathering and hissing across its broad surface, to founder in sizzling foam. The continuous roar as reinforcements flung more massed water on top of the reef. The swirlings and hissings and whisperings as minute by minute broken waves spilled farther across the reef and came creeping towards the Mound. The sobbings, the sighings and gurglings as eager, snaky arms gained the creek mouths and began rushing up. The gradually diminishing thunder as other waves fell on deepening water upon the reef to surge on over water into the creeks.

Then at last only a crooning murmur when the tide was full and the great reef quite drowned.

There were the very different sounds, too, the much more lonely sounds when on very windy nights a vast murmuring would come sighing over the island from the mangrove forest. In gusts, it would come, in sobbing shrieks that died away among the boulders. No wonder the legends of primitive man are full of ghostly things.

I spent a little of each night straightening out and hardening the spear prongs bent daily by the big fish. Knowing how to sharpen picks made the tempering of the soft wire easy. Otherwise, the prongs would have bent with every fish they struck. Surprising force is required to pierce the tough skin and scales of some fish. It must have been a wonderful discovery to stone-age man when he found that by slowly heating his wooden spear prongs in the fire he could make them very hard. In life, even the simplest thing has to be thought out or accidentally discovered, then, by repetition, done thoroughly before success is assured. To harden the prongs each night meant only to hammer them straight, heat them nearly dull hot, tip them a few seconds one inch deep in water, then plunge straight down and withdraw. It was a pleasure then to watch by fire-light the temper coming down, and know a good job well done. I was independent even of a file to sharpen the points, for this could be done with time and patience and heat and hammering and final grinding between two hard stones—or better still, by vigorous rubbing in a tiny groove of a huge boulder, water sparingly added.

One morning I was on top of the Mound when there was just sufficient wind to ripple the sombre waters and send a chill through the threadbare shirt. Later, clouds of drifting mist drove me farther in among the coldly sheltering rocks. About midday my heart jumped painfully; far out to sea was the blurred image of a mangrove-tree where a tree should never be. I leapt up, staring with thumping heart lest the shifting mists blot that tree from sight. A mangrove covered mud bank was to the east of the tree. Half an hour later the tree disappeared behind the bank. Oh, the joy! The "tree" was a moving sail beyond shadow of a doubt.

Which way was she travelling? She could not be a Japanese *beche-de-mer* cutter, for at that distance her sails would not be distinguishable. The ketch had the largest sails along that portion of the coast. But it would be best not to assume it was the ketch. Still, something told me that it was.

A little later it came from behind the mud bank and slowly grew into two blurred sails. Slowly they drew closer, gradually growing more distinct as the vessel that carried them drifted slowly west. She was coming straight from the mainland, from around Cape Melville, tacking east and west. That would bring her right here. It *was* the ketch!

The tide was on the turn; it would be some hours yet before I could run to Charlie with the news.

All that afternoon the ketch tacked east and west, ever coming closer, closer. Often, mists would hide her, but sooner or later she would appear again, ever more distinct. Towards sundown she showed up plainly, gliding behind an island about four miles away. She would anchor for the night. Now the sky had grown black. There was no sign of Charlie on the Peak. It sheltered his camp from the sea, so, as he rarely climbed it, he would not know the ketch was coming. Picturing his delight, I ran splashing along the drying reef. It was nearly sundown.

Charlie was crouched over his galley fire, eating fish. I was shocked— his unkempt hair and beard had grown so. His deep-sunk eyes had lost their wildness.

"Charlie! the ketch is coming!"

"How do you know?" he growled.

"Because I have been watching it all day." "Well, let it come."

"But it will take us off."

"It won't take *me* off."

"Yes it will, the weather is calm, a dinghy can land."

"No dinghy will land. Whether or not, they won't take me off."

I sat down.

"Don't you want to go?"

"No!"

"Heavens man! What is the matter with you?"

"Nothing is the matter with me."

"Well, I'm going. Thank heaven this is my last night on this wretched island."

He said nothing, just kept munching while staring into the fire. It was hard to know what to say. To all protestations, to every point of view, he only grunted in reply. I was too delighted to care a great deal, the ketch was there and Charlie would change his mind in the morning. Presently he stood up and walked into the tent, tying close the door. I was too absorbed by thought of the ketch to notice whether he was working up for a bad turn, or just recovering from one.

"Be ready in the morning," I called, "the tide will be out and I'll be over here at daylight. Have all your things ready in case a wind springs up after dawn."

"You attend to your own affairs and don't bother about mine!" he growled from the tent.

I walked back to the reef and the Mound, whistling cheerily. It was chilly, but through the mists stars at times shone brightly. Perhaps to-morrow would be a fine dawn. Occasionally a big crab scuttled across the reef. It was a pleasure to let them live. Sleep hardly came at all that night.

Before dawn I was gazing seaward from the Mound. There was no sign of the sun; sea and sky were overcast with swiftly travelling banks of black cloud. A light wind, icy cold, sent the chill breaths of ghostly sleet gusts through and through one. With the greying of dawn I hurried along the reef to the Peak.

Even from its summit visibility extended barely a mile to sea. Soon the sun would drive these blinding mists away.

An hour later and Charlie appeared noiselessly, glaring out to sea.

"Where are your blanket and things?" I cried.

"Won't want them. She won't land."

I could have kicked him.

"Of all the Jonahs I've ever met you are the worst," I protested. "Why won't she land?"

"Look at the weather."

"Looks black, but it's not rough yet. They'll land all right."

He sat down, staring out at the mists, his bony knees clasped nearly under his chin, his deep-lined face and haggard eyes a picture of brooding misery.

"A week in Cooktown and we won't know one another," I ventured. "How would a bath, a shave and clean clothes and a good feed at the West Coast Hotel go down now?"

"You're counting your chickens before they're hatched," he replied soberly.

We sat there silently.

An hour later and a weak, quavering shaft of light shot up over Lizard Island to be immediately swallowed by the mist. Charlie stood ' up, turned, and began climbing down the Peak on his camp side.

"Don't leave anything behind," I called—"not that we've got much to leave behind anyway."

He stopped and looked back, his expression more chilly than the mists. Then he turned and slowly descended the Peak.

"You'll just about get on the ketch in time, Charlie, me lad," I muttered. "It's a cot in hospital for you when we reach Cooktown. And for you too! Talking to yourself is the first stage."

I felt a bit frightened.

More rays of light came; stronger this time, more slowly swallowed up.

The mists began to lift away towards the mainland; the blanketing clouds began travelling towards the north. Then the crest of Lizard Island shot out from blackness illumined by a ball of shimmering light. Long, fiery arms shattered the mists into tremulous coils of fleecy vapour. Westward the mist was lifting. I yelled and waved as the ketch's two big sails stood out lily-white through the thinning mists. She was hardly three miles away, if that; her framework stood out plainly under a shaft of sunlight. But currents or drift must have taken her farther back; she was facing the island now and would pass it quite close if a wind did not spring up. I felt tempted to run back to the Mound but waited a while. She was barely moving; she was stationary now; the faint gusts of breeze had dropped to a calm. The sun shone in fitful bursts of light. Suddenly the sky darkened as black clouds rolled low down over the sea.

Then a breeze came; in a blaze of sunlight the sea rippled, and the ketch began to surge on— straight for the Mound. I could stand it no longer, but ran down the Peak and out on to the reef, running to the Mound. The ketch was forging down the channel, she would pass the Mound only a few hundred yards distant. I took off my tattered shirt and waved frantically. Then the cursed mists came down and blotted from view ketch and sea and everything. I yelled wildly knowing that the ketch would sheer away from the reef—a death-trap in the mists. Would she go straight on? She could not anchor; the water was too deep. With the great reef nearby and Coquet Island and other reefs, she was in a nasty position.

At last the mists cleared again, and there the ketch was a mile away from the Mound and heading towards Coquet Island. I could have howled. But what a relieved man the skipper must have been!

Near Coquet her sails came tumbling down and the anchor chain rattled companionably.

In brilliant sunlight I started to hurry back to the Peak when Charlie appeared, cautiously climbing the Peak. Even at that distance, something in his stealthy climb made me stay on top of the Mound and watch him. When near the top of the Peak he crouched and did not show himself. I wondered why. It didn't matter. The breeze had fallen to dead calm again, the ketch could not move. As soon as the tide began coming in she would send a dinghy ashore, timed so that it could row over the reef with the tide. We should be taken aboard and the ketch would drift away with the strengthening tide if there was no wind. It was almost unbearable, sitting there, waiting, staring towards the distant ketch as the mists came and went.

At last the tide began coming in. Faintly, came the distant rattle of pulley blocks. I jumped up ready to run along the reef to the lagoon. Up went the sails and slowly they filled. She was going to drift in with the tide as close to the island as she dared, then lower a dinghy.

Slowly the ketch began to creep ahead. I stood on a rock and waved the last of my shirt. But again the mist came down and blotted out Coquet Island, blotted out the ketch, blotted - out the sea. How I cursed it!

Slowly the mist lifted. And there were the big sails of the ketch bellying under a growing breeze. Miserably I saw the jib sail tautened out where the stern should be. The ketch was sailing south on the return tack to Cooktown.

All the yelling, all the arm waving in the world would not bring her back.

Long afterwards I met the skipper, and he explained that Charlie had definitely instructed him that there would be no need to send a boat ashore unless a well-defined signal called him. Otherwise, he was to know that some passing *beche-de-mer* boat had picked us up or left us more provisions. Charlie had brought lots of vegetable seeds in his swag. He meant to start a garden, to keep fowls and to bring goats from Cooktown. His idea was to be utterly cut off from and independent of the world." Why he had shown me the tin specimens and encouraged me to go with him, I never learned. His oversight in forgetting his 'scope and chemicals in Cooktown had no doubt deranged both his plan and his reasoning.

I nearly went crazy when the ketch sailed away. To save reason I picked up the old Malay's log book of the *Sea Foam*, and, as the days drifted past, jotted down the diary from which this story is written.

I erected a flag of distress up on the Lookout, sacrificing the precious blanket, keeping only the rug. The flagpole was a long bamboo washed among the rocks. A cairn was already erected. I worked for hours making it still higher; then lashed the blanket to the bamboo flagpole and buried its butt deep in the cairn. Any breeze would turn the blanket into a flag visible far away. Passing steamers and pearling luggers could not fail to see it.

An occasional vessel saw it—and passed on to my bitter, bitter disappointment. I did not realize that the flag was taken for that of a *beche-de-mer* fishing station. There were a few such up along the coast. The cutters would bring their fish to their island depot to be smoke cured. They would load with wood and water; then the vessel would sail away to its fishing-grounds. The men or man on the island would later signal from a hill when he was ready to cure more fish, or when some other vessel of the fleet had called in with supplies. A flag like that, high upon a peak, is visible for many miles to sea. Several steamer captains and pearling men long afterwards told me that they had seen the signal and had (very naturally in such circumstances) put it down to a *beche-de-mer* station signalling her cutters away out on the Great Barrier Reef.

16

The Shark

The kerosene tin bucket and billy cans were empty. A glance at the sky, at the gathering clouds low down, a sniff of the – moisture laden air, hinted that it might rain soon. But a man must be sure of water. I trudged along the reef at low tide, then into the mangroves at the foot of the Peak, walking quite soundlessly, barefooted, over the roots and mud, staring among the mangroves ahead and to the right and left. How quickly a civilized man becomes instinctively primitive! Put him in the environment, and sleeping instincts naturally awake. It was no hint of danger that urged me put the cans down when within a hundred yards of the well and creep stealthily forward. And no conscious thought warned that the birds were silent when on this hot day they should have been bathing and chirping around the well. I peered from between the twisted forks of a tree. There the ring of stones that formed the lip of the well; the dry shells and coral strewn there must be quite warm. But no birds were splashing in the cool water; their uneasy flutterings and chirping complaints were coming from somewhere deep among the trees surrounding the well.

So Charlie was on the rampage again!

So was I, with a quick, mad feeling. Cautiously I worked back among the mangroves, then, bending while jumping from root to root, quickly reached the reef and ran round the seaward side of the Peak and so to the lagoon and Charlie's camp. The fire was banked as usual, the tent door neatly closed. Seizing a firestick I whirled it around until it blazed then broke into the tent, throwing the firestick at the walls then throwing Charlie's few things to safety outside. As the tent blazed up I ran up the tiny divide, then crawled amongst the grass and peered over the top. Charlie was already racing up the path from the well waving his toy gun at the smoke and yelling like mad. He panted straight past and plunged at the burning tent. Running down the path to the well I quickly filled the buckets, had a long drink, grasped the buckets, and hurried away for the reef and the Mound.

Charlie was forcing me to live like an animal among the rocks. Now he would have to find a den for himself or else build a gunyah. But when I'd reached the Mound and hidden the water, the warmth of triumph wore off. The position was serious. If every time Charlie went crazy he was to lie in ambush at the well, then one of us must go under sometime. It might be a long time yet. He only went really mad at the height of his bad spells; during such periods I might have water stored at the Mound. But sooner or later, if we were marooned here long enough, we must clash at the well. It was almost impossible to watch him continuously and at the same time keep the water cans filled, because both the mangrove forest and the tiny ridge hid each camp from the other. When the tide was in it completely separated us; when it was out by day each of us had to fish to live. In the mangroves we might be prowling a mile apart or only a few yards, each unseen by the other. If at low tide I trespassed on Charlie's country by climbing the Peak and, from that vantage point, failed to see him, it would be impossible to tell whether he was in the mangroves fishing, or hiding by the well, or lying asleep, or brooding in his camp. The hardest part of it all was the utter absurdity of it—two lonely men on a barren island fighting one another.

Gloomy thoughts these as I picked up the fish spear and entered the mangrove forest—savage thoughts too.

Right into the black heart of the great' sea swamp, over patches of coral sand and acres of thick black mud matted with a network of roots. Never slipping on the bow-shaped roots, never treading on a rotten one or those deceptive ones that will not bear weight, stepping surely onward, now and again ducking head or shoulders naturally and unconsciously under fantastic branches that drooped lower than their fellows. Whether in desert or jungle, man will soon grow into the life he must live to keep alive. In places here were tree-sheltered inlets holding long quiet pools. Some were cross- able by bridges of slime-encrusted tree trunks, washed by mighty storms from the distant mainland. The laws and vagaries of the coming and going tides had brought them across the sea, then floated them over the reef and swept them along these twisting water lanes among the trees. Perhaps the seas in ages past have populated whole island systems that way, swept canoe loads of people many miles out of their course to cast them upon some uninhabited island. Just as the sea with its flotsam and jetsam has made thousands of islands, as even to-day it is washing the seeds of plants and trees to thousands of island shores. Walking in this gloomy silence a man stepped silent as a shadow, with eyes ceaselessly peering to right and left, down at the mud and into every pool of water. Bare feet on moist tree roots make no sound, leave no track.

Often a hideous head would wave from below the mangrove roots as the needle-toothed snout of a sea eel poked out from its burrow. Nearly always the heads of these sea eels swayed to and fro, their eyes like shiny beads. Sometimes the bones of fish would lie before their burrows. Always hideous were these heads, swaying as if gasping open-mouthed like many fanged serpents.

It was surprising how far one could see between the myriad trunks, merely by the tiniest movement of the head. A stranger in this labyrinth would flounder desperately in the mud and become entangled in the roots, his vision limited to yards. An eerie world—the smell of mud and water and vegetation over everything; the sharp pistol-like reports of a bursting mangrove pod, and an unexplainable sound, far away. Then a slow, sucking movement here and there in the mud. Watch it for minutes and a mud bubble slowly rises, tremulous as it grows. It gradually subsides, or else rises until it bursts with a "plop," ejecting gas from the miniature crater. No doubt these eruptions are caused by decaying fish or vegetable matter.

Sometimes came the ghostly "whispering" of thousands of tiny crabs as they moved like a living, rustling carpet all around the strange intruder. That carpet emitted the softest hissings, hundreds and hundreds of them, merging into one sound. And as it moved, thousands of tiny eyes glared up, thousands of tiny claws were raised menacingly. The moving mass constantly opened at the centre as I stepped forward and as constantly closed in as I passed. It moved with me effortlessly as a mass, yet each tiny crab moved individually. To step smartly forward meant that a lane would open sharply with clinkings of tightly-packed shells as the crabs scurried aside from feet that would tramp them down. Sometimes at night on the Mound I used to shudder at the thought of a man becoming crippled in the mangroves and one of these "carpets" finding him.

I halted a moment at a favourite channel, gazing at the shallow water. A fish darted past, another followed, speeding swiftly in among a clump of roots. Others like ghostly shades sped by. This activity was strange, for the water had not been disturbed. A big spotted bream was lying uneasily between two roots, head turned upstream. With a sudden swirl of the tail it was gone downstream, a fleeting streak. Now a fine cod came swimming swiftly down the channel, his big blunt head rippling the water. Instantly I threw, then leapt into the water, snatching at the spear haft as the impaled fish struggled to tear it away.

A sudden swishing noise and I jumped for the mangrove roots, the water hissing as I sprang for the branches and glanced behind. Instinctive terror had caused that wild spring. The fin of a shark cut the pool as the monster snapped right and left at fish that darted from every quarter of the hole.

My thigh was stinging and the worn pants were torn away. What looked a nasty gash accounted for the stinging. It was a frightening moment; a man can be deadly scared when he is hurt and quite alone. Visions of a poisoned wound from the mangrove mud brought a. sickly feeling. Really, the shark's teeth had merely grazed the leg, but it looked bad enough at the time and in the circumstances. Tearing otf the shirt I made a hasty bandage, tightening it with a mangrove stick until the rotten cloth tore. The wound began to throb and pain, then began to bleed profusely. I hurried back towards the Mound, fearing that loss of blood might cause faintness, and that the tide, swirling in, would trap me amongst the mangroves. The Mound had never seemed so far away; but I limped out of the mangroves at last and thankfully breathed in the open air and gazed on the sky and the sea. After a rest thirst came. As I hobbled forward again, the leg was stiff and throbbing. Badly scared, I crawled up over the boulders to where the cool water lay hidden. The heat from those granite boulders made a man feel faint. It was a job to lever away the flat stone that covered the water.

The bucket and billy cans were filled with sand!

Charlie laughed from away below, his shaggy head peering over, a rock. He leapt up and ran along the reef, hurrying to beat the tide just beginning to turn. Again and again came his laughter.

I was too startled, too dazed to shout. If he had known of my plight he would surely have returned. This was his revenge for the burning of his tent. There would be no chance of getting water now until morning when the tide was out.

I crawled away under the nearest stunted tree on the mangrove side of the Mound, raving at what a stupid fool Charlie was. His revenge would perhaps have been sensible enough if a man hadn't been hurt. Very slowly the sun went down behind the hazy mainland, lighting up the peaks of the distant ranges with a dim splendour. A whispering wind sprang suddenly from the south-east. The calm sea black-green, in quick answer broke into curly tops of creamy foam. The short twilight came; stars peeped out; little Coquet blinked sympathetically. That cool wind was heaven sent.

Now a veil of blackest velvet crept over the stars. A murmuring began to grow far away in the mangrove tops. It gathered strength, then came moving on, fast growing louder. Soon the wind began to howl in fitful gusts among the rocks. It was late in the night when the first raindrops fell with soft, clinging splashes. When they came, ice-cold, I crawled down to the billy cans, emptied them of sand, and smiled up at the sky.

Wind whistled far back among the mangroves, gradually swelling into a shriek as the vast canopy of foliage shuddered to the blast's fury. The surf on the reef grew into a booming roar. Sheets of blinding rain lashed in from the massed darkness above the sea. Shivering, I crept to the big flat rock. The crevice was already filling with rain-water! That was a wonderful drink. Before dawn, bucket and billies and crevice were full.

17

The Crabs

Next morning the sun shone brightly with that clear, warmth-giving light of the Cape York Peninsula mornings. Pools of water glistened in every depression in the rocks. The leg was dreadfully stiff. I crept down into the den, fearful lest the banked-up fire might have smothered itself. But the ashes were comfortingly warm. Tearing up a strip of bark and crushing it into fibre was the work of a moment, similarly to scrape away the ashes, place the fibre in the hot middle, bend down and blow. Tiny sparks flew up among the ashes; soon the fibre blazed, and presently a crackling fire warmed the den. It was a cheery triumph; already I felt better. The company of fire to a lonely man is wonderful, especially when he is sick.

There was plenty of fresh water, the fire was here, everything was quite all right. Suddenly I thought of the fish spear! The precious iron prongs had been carried away by the impaled fish yesterday. That memory was a jolt—from the iron age back to the wood at one blow. Still, the fire crackled companionably. Wooden spear prongs, just as the aboriginals fashion them, must replace iron for the time being. Hopeless, though, to walk through the mangroves to find and spear fish until the leg got better—a few days at least. Crabs! Crabs and shell-fish. Impossible to starve.

The world was a cheery place again. It could have been much worse. Now for the job of crawling up the crevice and limping back with a billy can of water. To bathe the wound was the main thing now. That wash in fresh salt water yesterday had stung it cruelly; but a salted wound was better than a poisoned leg. Soon the billy boiled and a long bathing of the wound brought considerable relief. Whistling, I hobbled to the patch of scrub and carefully selected a slender but strong stick eight feet long, then a much thinner one. From these would be fashioned a spear. As I threw them down the crevice and went for a billy can of water, dismay came; the few rock pools already showed signs of evaporation. This meant pains-taking labour in sheltering the precious holes with flat rocks. The handful of little local birds were amusingly indignant for they had claimed the water to bathe in. But they could fly to the well; I told them so when they scolded me. After a searching gaze across the sunlit sea I crawled down into the den, poked the spear sticks into the ashes of the fire, and stretched back to rest the leg.

I fell asleep, to awake and see stars glinting like softest gold down through the black rock crevice. And hunger came. Then began work that grew more interesting as the night wore on, the fire humming cheery encouragement. Blessing the precious pocket knife, I cut the smaller stick into four eighteen-inch lengths, carefully making the points long and tapering, but not too thin, for a long thin point snaps off easily, becomes burred with one throw should it miss the fish and hit coral or a root. After the sharpening, the prongs were thrust into hot ashes with the butts just protruding so that each could be continually turned. Then began the paring down of the long haft of the spear- to-be, the wood being shaved and scraped so that the balance of weight would start at about eighteen inches from the spear head. The prongs, when eventually bound to the spear head, would project another twelve inches. Thus the haft weight, being nearly two feet behind the prong tips, would lend balance and accuracy, and give distance with weight, to the spear throw. What a fix would a man have been in had he not keenly watched the aboriginal spear makers at work! Those beetle-browed old experts had a lifetime of practice and un-limited leisure, for the young warriors of the tribe eagerly brought them food in part payment for those perfectly made weapons. But I was a civilized man and would be very hungry on the morrow. For countless generations their ancestors had been trained to make out of wood weapons that would kill animals. A modern man was not even in the kindergarten class. They would have laughed uproariously at this attempt!

I balanced the haft again and again, paring away a little here, a little there; it presently began to take shape. Continuously turning the prongs in the ashes, heaping hotter ashes around them, I wondered the while how long it took the first aboriginals to discover the wood most suitable for their spears, the many differences and qualities in soft, medium, and hard woods; to learn the laws of length, straightness, weight, and balance; to learn that heat properly applied, will straighten and toughen wood, make infinitely better weapons. How long did it take them to evolve their different spears, fish and animal and war? How much longer then, to learn that a bone or stone point was superior in cutting and lasting qualities to wood? And who, at long last, was the genius who thought out and made the womera, that lever which lends a spear so much greater accuracy, distance, and striking power than when thrown by hand? Only when a man sits down to make a stone-age weapon does he realize the thought and craftsmanship that, through centuries, must have gone into the production of these weapons.

When the haft was shaped, I spread out ashes and buried it in them, continually turning it all through the night, heaping hotter ashes here and there in constant endeavour to straighten and toughen it. To harden it, especially the prongs, requires a long and slow process that time would not allow, nor was the wood suitable. A shaft of light creeping down the crevice surprisingly heralded the coming of a new dawn; the night had flown indeed. The fire was burning soberly. A receding murmur from the reef told that the tide was racing out to sea. I bound the four prongs to the haft tip, using a torn strip from the blanket and fixing each prong so that the four tips were spread just two inches from each other. Thus the aboriginals, thousands of years ago, anticipated one great difference between our shot-gun and rifle. A rifle carries much farther than a shot-gun propelling one straight bullet that must hit to kill. The shot-gun carries only a short distance but its many pellets spread out, lending a much greater chance of hitting the object with some at least of the pellets. So with the aboriginals' war and hunting and fish spears. The war spear can be thrown farther, but its one point must hit the object. The fish spear with its four prongs will not travel nearly so far, but the spread of its four prongs gives it four chances, though only one of those prongs is needed to pierce a fish.

These prongs of mine were none too hard but they must serve for the time being. I crawled up the crevice eager to try this weapon fashioned by my own hand. In gold and flame the sun had already sprung up over the sea. By a distant sand-bank several toy handkerchiefs were revealed by the growing light. *Beche-de- mer* cutters, already at work out towards the Great Barrier Reef. If only lack of water would bring them to the island! If they only knew water was here! It was useless wishing. They would sail to the mainland for water, knowing well the difficulty of landing on this island except in calm weather. Sea roamers all of them, here to-day, gone to-morrow.

My leg being a bit sore and stiff, I used a forked stick as a crutch to hobble down to the reef. After a while the leg grew warm, and much easier. A good meal, would work wonders.

Some rocks at the sea edge were encrusted with small oysters, inviting a man to crush many shells with a stone; but this scanty repast was barely an appetizer. Numerous spiky shellfish fleshed in vivid red and green lay in shallow pools. A dubious looking meal these, but it might be advisable to lay some on the rocks and later to cook and try them. A future serious accident or illness might nail me to the Mound beyond hope of seeking fish or crabs. Should such disaster come, edible shell-fish within a few yards of the Mound might be precious. The urge to live and primitive environment makes a man think ahead.

Had I only known it, there were plenty of edible shell-fish out on the reef. The muscles of the big clams even though tough are quite eatable, despite the poisonous looking fringe.

It was a thousand yards' walk along the reef to the foot of the Peak where the crab colony lived in its gloomy corner of the mangrove edge. That ledge of dead coral just within the mangrove edge was really their battlements, and within that wall they had their burrows. A beautiful day, the grass golden on the sides of the Peak; the flag pole stood up there outlined sharp as a needle, its flag of distress bravely flapping in a light breeze. Big clams showered their water sprays as I hobbled along, little crabs scuttled into pools in which were big black *beche-de-mer* like crinkly gnomes among fairy gardens of seaweeds and coral. Along the edge of the reef a black fin moved effortlessly. Oh for a rifle to smash the beastly thing. It kept exact pace with me along the edge of the reef, neither gliding one yard ahead nor following one yard behind.

I crouched low when near the crab colony, for those horny-plated fellows would scamper towards their burrows the moment they saw danger—not right into their burrows but near enough for a quick bolt to safety. There they would watch, edging inch by inch nearer their burrows as I approached foot by foot. Those crabs knew me.

Peering from the butt of a mangrove-tree I surveyed my prospective breakfast. Half a dozen big green fellows were down at the water's edge industriously hunting for *their* breakfast while other big blue fellows were straddling across the coral between the water and the burrows; still others were foraging among the mangrove roots for small shell-fish in the mud— one with his enormous claws was crushing a shell. Several were half in and half out of their burrows, leisurely regarding the scenery.

Two big fellows commenced to quarrel, circling round each other with claws menacingly open and stretched out over their "heads," grotesquely suggestive of crouching wrestlers. One reached out swiftly; but the other slid aside, jerking his claws well back as a boxer might leap aside with raised arms to ward off a blow. The coral pebbles rattled from their slithering legs and shells as each sought to grip the other's claw, keeping their softer bellies to the ground while presenting to the other the tough shell of their backs. Suddenly, one sprang, rearing swiftly as he tried to heave his claws over the back of the other; but this fellow reared too and they clashed ineffectively, reeling apart, crouching again. Other crabs were watching, several warily edging closer as if anxious to join in. With a spring the fighters clinched, hard shell rattling on shell, claws clashing with the vicious snap of steel traps. One claw was shorn straight off at a joint; it rattled on the coral while the wounded crab fought desperately with the remaining claw to regain its burrow. The other fiercely pressed his advantage, warding off attack with one claw while snapping for a grip to crush his adversary's "head" with the other. As I sprang forward they reared up, fighting as stallions might, striving to tear each other to pieces. One swift thrust and the spear prongs had impaled both crabs. There was a scraping rattle of hard shells on coral as the onlookers vanished.

I was thrilled with the spear; then immediately saw that the prongs had penetrated the tender underneath parts of the crabs when they had reared up. Still, so much the better, for if the prongs had penetrated the hard upper shells the points would have been burred.

The walk back to the Mound was a pleasure, and I remembered to collect the shell-fish on the way. The billy was soon boiled, the crabs cooked and hungrily eaten while the shell-fish were cooking. It really would be wise to eat several and learn if they were good for food. The possibility of becoming ill and incapable of moving far from the Mound for food had taken a strong hold. But the eating of those fish later in the afternoon brought on violent sickness.

That evening, partially recovered from fright and sickness, I sat up on the Mound looking across at Coquet. The cheery little light would flash a moment then vanish, to flash again just when expected. It seemed to come round and flash just for me.

Great company.

18

The Sweet Potatoes

All count of days and weeks was lost. Time just drifted on. When the tide was out was the time to fish, when the tide was in was sleeping time if night; if day, there was nothing to do but sit' up on the Mound or Peak and gaze out to sea. From the Peak Charlie's camp was plainly visible; he had built quite a good one from odds and ends of wreckage, apparently, with the roof neatly thatched with grass. The mere burning of a tent meant only a spasm of anger to Charlie. His camp looked a great deal more inviting than a hole in the rocks.

One day he emerged from the mangroves, threw his fish down by the galley fire and moved about camp quite normally. I determined to visit him—for company's sake and to ask for some wire for the spear. The job of constantly fashioning new points and hardening them was so tedious and the spears were so inefficient that each day brought a struggle to secure sufficient fish to live. Failures occurred so frequently. The prongs would not always penetrate the scales and skin, which meant hesitation in attempting to spear a large fish. To hold anything over a five-pound fish was impossible, even when, luckily, the prongs pierced it. To spear a fish did not always mean to secure it; for the fish invariably put up a violent struggle and stood a good chance of wrenching away from an inefficient weapon. More than once, the very first throw of the day had been a miss and the points had burred against roots or coral. I longed for iron prongs.

So one morning 1 walked along the reef, then turned inland towards Charlie's camp and saw him at the foot of the Peak near the mangrove edge, on the one tiny, flat, loamy spot on the island. He was bending among the long grass apparently working. He was tending sweet potato plants, their vivid green in orderly rows well-hidden and hedged all around by the tall grass. They must be the plants he had sown—it seemed months ago now. A famishing feeling came over me. Without bread for a long time, living only on fish and crabs, the thought of those potatoes was almost overwhelming.

He looked up, then bent again to his weeding.

"They look good!" I nodded enthusiastically.

"Not bad," he growled. "They're coming on well."

"I never dreamt you could make such a good garden out of this tiny place."

"A man can do a lot with unpromising material if he sets his mind to it."

"What surprises me is that I've sat up on that Peak and never noticed the garden down here."

"A man seldom sees what's under his nose."

"You've worked a miracle anyway. I don't remember when I've ever seen sweet potatoes look so well."

Charlie straightened up and with the pride of the true gardener gazed reflectively at the plants.

"They *have* come on well. They'll last for months now. With this garden a man need not worry about being out of flour. I've got some pumpkin and melon seeds too. If a man only had a few goats he could easily keep himself in meat. And fowls would find plenty to live on in this island. There's insects among the grass and seeds. Fowls would soon get to rooting along the mangrove edges at high water. Plenty of shrimps and water grubs in the mud there. And they could tackle shell-fish too, break them with their beaks against a stone like wild birds do."

"Plenty of eggs then."

"They'd lay like clockwork."

We poked about among the plants, admiring them. Mine was a hungry admiration, though a genuine one. Charlie was pleased because he was a born gardener. He had planned this garden long ago, had planted it and quietly tended it and seen it come to fruition. He bent down and scraped the rich black loam from the roots of a plant, exposing the pink young tubers. I tingled.

"They won't be ready for the pot for another ten days. When they are, you'd better come along and dig some."

"With pleasure," I accepted enthusiastically. "That day cannot come too soon."

"Take them from wherever you see I've taken them," he directed, "then the rows will grow evenly. And plant the vines again where you take the tubers from. We'll have them continually growing then for months on end, as we dig one row we'll have automatically planted another, and so on."

"Right-oh, I'll dig 'em properly. This garden is going to make a great difference."

"It is. Helps make life liveable and gives a man something to think of."

"How's your fishing?"

"Not bad. Have to push farther out over the island though, as I fish the smaller creeks out."

"I've found the same thing. Lots of the fish seem to make their home in the one creek. As they get killed or hunted out the creek becomes bare of fish except for strays brought in by the tide."

"Yes."

"I'm finding it dashed awkward now, though. A while back a big fish got away with my wire prongs and it's been a wretched job ever since trying to spear them with wooden prongs."

"There's plenty of wire hooks at the camp. Come and get some."

"Good-oh."

Those iron prongs were going to be more precious than gold.

We strolled yarning back to his camp. But what a shock a stranger would have got had he landed on the island and come face to face with Charlie. His tangled, wiry beard was black and grey, his moustache ragged and long, his thatch of iron-grey hair hung down over deep-set eyes. A grimly set mouth. The remains of a shirt and trousers exposed long hairy limbs burned black from sun and spray. Bareheaded, with big bare feet, Charlie looked the wild man. I wondered how frightening I looked.

We yarned at the camp until the incoming tide forced a return to the Mound. It was a very cheerful return though, with a gloating backward glance towards the hidden potato patch. Some strange freak of memory brought back Palestine, and snipers lying so close and still in the barley fields that a man might actually walk on one before he saw him. And on this tiny speck, on the one wee patch of loamy soil, long grass had shielded a bed of growing sweet potatoes. The sun went down and quietness came. That was a happy evening! —in the den with the fire burning brightly, busy straightening four wire hooks into four prongs, the "tap-tap-tap" on the stone anvil a businesslike accompaniment to the job on hand. Then sharpening the points, tempering them, and binding them expertly to the spear haft. The day of the amateur was just about finished now. Tomorrow's fishing would be a pleasure; it would be a lucky fish that escaped. A pleasure too in the thought that while Charlie was all right we could enjoy a yarn every day. Time would fly now, what with a yarn and iron spear prongs and sweet potatoes to look forward to. And it would be a good idea to go every day to the well and keep my water bucket and billy cans full to the brim with water. I had felt sorely tempted to suggest that we camp in company again, but second thoughts had counselled that we should get along better if we remained as we were. Charlie would inevitably succumb to another wild turn. That night, dreams were wonderful; dreams of feasts of boiled sweet potatoes. Next morning the tide was not right out when I dived into the mangroves, new spear in hand. The balance of the thing was company, the iron prongs gave entire confidence. And this was going to be an exploring day; for the fish in the nearby creeks were rapidly thinning out. Pools that had been alive with fish now sheltered only one or two hunted specimens here and there. The big crabs at the colony were not so plentiful either; and there seemed to be only one colony. It would be disastrous if they were killed out, or if the cunning brutes migrated.

Numerous fish apparently lived in the mangroves and seldom ventured out to sea, preferring the easy life when the tide was out, the security of the mangrove roots when the tide came swirling in with voracious hunters from the open sea. Life for them out there would mean ceaseless warfare.

With time and experience and keenness, it had become natural to distinguish these fish. There was the flat butter-fish that always leant its mottled body against the mottled roots of a particular tree; the big, browny-black cod that had its den within the big, twisted, browny-black roots of a dark-barked mangrove. There was the individual fish (with a piece bitten out of the tail) that was always to be seen in its own particular pool; the fish with some particular marking distinguishing it; and the fish whose snout was to be seen poking out from below , some particular submerged log. Practically every pool held its big cod that, because of its size, could safely stay in the open upon the cleanest patch of sand.

The beastly eels clung to their particular burrows; but these were all individual burrows quite unlike the crab colony. The burrow of an eel was to be found strategically placed among the roots in the edge of a pool. An occasional big crab, explorer or outcast prowled about in the depths of the mangroves, his dull green, or shadowy purple, or heavy blue shell merging so well with the mud and roots that, unless he foolishly moved, it was only by chance you saw him. These pugnacious marauders were bushrangers among their kind, though when cornered they invariably put up a fight against man or monster fish.

Easy to tell, too, the "outside" fish that had come in with the tide and remained too long. Such a fish would frantically swim downstream, only to be turned back by a sand-bank and whizz past me back up the pool; there it would turn and torpedo down again in futile efforts to reach the main creek and the open sea. Regular denizens knowing that such escape was impossible, would simply dive into the tangle of roots lining the pool, and pressing themselves against a root, lie still and camouflaged. So well aware were they of the protection of immobility that some would allow a spear to be thrust twice at them without moving.

But experience teaches. Given an iron-pronged spear I now seldom missed—except when throwing at a cruising fish. To throw just ahead of those swiftly moving ripples, and hit the unseen mark is very different to spearing stationary prey, even when marvellously camouflaged and protected by a network of roots. An entirely different throw and aim was necessary too. Instead of aiming just behind, a man had to aim just ahead of the fish, that is ahead of the faint ripples that were made on the surface by his speeding snout below. When the tide was in, this big ocean forest swarmed with fish of every type; determined, ravenous brutes no matter what their size. Savage fights took place then throughout the submerged forest, often to be plainly heard up on the Mound. But the mangrove fish must have been comparatively safe under the maze of mangrove roots while incoming fish sought and fought for them in such unnatural environment. Butting against such obstacles many a fish with battered snout must gladly have made his way back to sea.

I went easily on into the still, silent heart of the mangroves. Rotted logs and stumps lay in the mud, bored through and through with the tunnels of the ship-worm. Funny little hoppy fish with big, comical eyes (for all the world like mischievous golliwogs) climbed the mangrove roots or went skipping over the mud. These quaint things can breathe in the air as well as in water. Now and again a long mangrove pod dropped down into the mud, its baby root landing first. The tide would carry it away to be washed on to some lonely island, there to grow into a mangrove-tree. Fiddler crabs backed away, making a fighting bluff with one big red claw raised menacingly above a little one. Quaggy pools were underfoot, sometimes a patch of pale blue mud had to be warily approached. This was "quick" mud—slimy, sticky stuff possessed of some horrible sucking power that could drag a man down. To follow up the muddy creeks where possible was the best way; otherwise, to step crouching over the twisted roots which so often covered acres. Imperceptibly the gloom lightened, faint daylight appeared among the trunks ahead. In surprise I stepped into easily the largest creek I'd yet seen, lined by far the tallest trees. On one of these, high up, was a rough platform of big sticks, and standing on it were two white-breasted sea eagles. Masters of all they surveyed, they glared contemptuously down. It was a pleasure to look at them. They were something new and interesting; something that shared the island with Charlie and me and the birds and fish and crabs and the sea. Up above was the open sky. This wide creek was a succession of long shallow pools, both mud- and sand-lined, with here and there a solemn crane at the water's edge, and with others perched on the trees. A shadow glided just under water; an enormous stingray, with small, pig-like eyes, its broad "wings" gently undulating, its whip-like tail slowly waving, the bony sting fully six inches long. A terrible thing to come lashing a man's leg! Let a man step on that fat, slimy body half-buried in the sand and the whip-like tail would lash up and around him and the poison sting pierce like a knife.

These pools, because they were long and wide and thus free of roots except at the edges, were the home of stingrays of all colours and sizes. Tiny "smoke clouds" were drifting up through the water where the brutes were slowly nosing the sand, burrowing for shell-fish, while others slowly glided by. Here and there on the pool bottoms they lay almost buried, their snouts and wings lightly covered with sand, just portions of their whip tails visible.

These would be treacherous pools to fish in. Probably this big creek twisted right across the heart of the island; possibly its outlet was the big creek mouth where Charlie and I had chased the turtle. Overhead here as if coming down from the clear sky was a murmur in the air of the sea pounding the distant reef. In the slime lay decaying logs like huge crocodiles dreaming in the mud of some bygone age. From the mangrove edge I searched (as far as visibility allowed) every log lest here might be the home of some real crocodile.

Time was speeding by. It would be pretty awful to be caught in a place like this by the tide. Cautiously I crossed the creek, prodding the spear into the sand and mud ahead, watched by the eagles and cranes. Now and again a stingray glided away and it was temptation to hurl the spear into the broad, flat back. But such a target would have departed with a swirl and carried the precious iron prongs with it.

Into the mangroves on the opposite side—and silence. A dense forest here, the visibility only a few yards. Here the roots grew much taller, the creeks were "steeper" and much fewer, but there appeared to be fish in all—fish that stared up without moving, that never before had been disturbed by man. It must be a long way back to the sea. This walk proved there were unlimited fish on the island; one could never starve even though one fished out creek after creek. The mangroves were almost impenetrable, necessitating a continuous crouching over the roots. An eerie feeling crept over me there in the gloom among that jungle of roots; nothing to see but a twisted maze of grotesque shapes; nothing to smell but mud; nothing to hear but a silence that became intense with listening. But there was seething, creeping, crawling life everywhere. Hidden mangrove birds were staring from behind leaf and trunk. There were insects in the mangrove leaves, and boring things in the trunks. With intense concentration, a man could distinguish tiny flakes like grains of falling powder. This finest sawdust was kicked out by the legs or tail of something boring into a mangrove branch. Put your ear to the branch, and you would hear the tiny thuds, or the tiny sawing as the insect within bored deeper. By mischance, you might easily get the grains of sawdust kicked in your eye. I wondered at the Power that had made all the life that was teeming in this mud forest. But it certainly was no place for a man. I hurried back, meeting the incoming tide half way, and emerged on the great broad reef under the open sky none too soon. It was glorious to breathe the fresh air and gaze across the sea and climb the Mound away from the waters that were now pouring into the mangroves.

19

The Deathtrap

The next ten days passed by cheerily—the fishing was easy, there was plenty of time to enjoy a long yarn with Charlie. He was his old self again and cheerfully retailed his little adventures on his own side of the island. He had discovered creeks, and reef pools that were storehouses of treasure to anyone interested in marine things. He had located the homes of big gropers far away along the reef and had a great tussle with a dugong that swam in to browse on the sea-grass where we had seen the turtle. He tried to manhandle the big sea cow in the shallow water, but it simply grunted and bowled him over; and when he got on to its back again and hung on to its flippers, it rolled him into the sand and grass nearly smothering him. He had found, too, the remnants of an old wreck all overgrown by coral, its dim shape only visible at very low water. One day he had an awful experience. He was far in among the mangroves with the tide just about to turn when his foot slipped among the roots and down he went with one leg in the air. He was trapped; his foot had gone straight down between the resilient roots which snapped tight again, gripping above his ankle. His other foot was high up upon the tight-packed roots. He had an awful job getting it down level, scared lest it become trapped too. After an hour's striving he freed himself; he would have been done had he lost his head. I could imagine him, sprawled there in an awkward position while with the haft of the spear and his hands he carefully and methodically strained to lever open the roots, sweating when he heard the first faint hissings and gurglings of the returning tide. He got free only just in time. As it was, he was quickly driven to the highest roots. He reached the outer mangroves by clawing from branch to branch, the water tugging at his waist.

One afternoon Charlie was not at camp, though the fire was lit and his fish cleaned and ready for the coals. Hanging on a branch were his old shorts recently patched with canvas from tin bags. When just about to shout I saw him through the mangroves out in the lagoon, lying upon the flat rock. It would be advisable to avoid Charlie for the next few days.

Back at the Mound I made a serious discovery. One of the billy cans was leaking—not leaking really, but there was the first sign of it —a tiny pin-hole in the bottom.

This was serious. All these flimsy things of civilization, the billy cans and the kerosene tin, would decay in time. That would mean the collapse of the reservoir. A more permanent one must be thought out. A glance towards the reef, and the problem was solved. Out there were big empty bailer and helmet and other shells, once the home of giant shell-fish. Some of those shells would hold more water than a billy can and were indestructible, unless purposely smashed. Any one of the giant clam shells would have held buckets of water; but all contained live fish, and it was impossible to chop them from the reef except with a tomahawk, and perhaps a crowbar. But the bailer and helmet shells would do, and when the cooking billy wore out they could be used for cooking pots too. The real billy cans and kerosene tin could then be kept only for carry the water from the well. Thus they'd last months longer.

Months! Heavens! Not a sail was in sight on the sea.

By sundown I had a fine collection of big shells spread out in rows. It was a pleasure to collect them and gloat on what a reservoir they would make. Two reservoirs. The old hiding place for one, and a secret reservoir, just in case anything happened to the first. What an ass a man was not to have thought of and used the shells before. It was becoming easier and easier to understand how primitive man lives so well without civilization. For all his simple needs Nature places the material ready to hand. All Man has to do is to think about it, then fashion from the materials provided just what he wants.

The next morning I walked along the reef bound for the Lookout up on the Peak and saw Charlie disappearing over the tiny ridge towards his camp, bowed under a load of something.

Potatoes! He had been digging potatoes.

Only for a moment I hesitated. He would be mad if I dug any while he had one of his bad turns. But he had said to take some when ripe—and, hang it all, they were ripe and I was ravenous.

I ran back to the Mound, jumped down the crevice, seized the tattered blanket and hurried back along the reef to the garden. The earth was all freshly turned where Charlie had been digging. And what potatoes they were! Big fat tubers with tender pink skins and delicious sweet-buk odour. I dug a lot and piled them on the blanket, replanted the vines, then hurried back to the Mound and filled the billy with potatoes.

It was a glorious meal, sweet potatoes boiled in fresh sea-water—and the billy refilled and simmering so that there would be plenty more potatoes ready to be eaten throughout the after-noon, as hunger dictated. On this red-letter day there would be no fishing. I stretched out on the warm granite rocks up on the Mound and stared lazily at the fleecy clouds, drifting here, there, everywhere and melting into the un-guessable heights of the infinite blue. Far up, circled a clear-cut miniature, majestic in its perfect mastery of the sky, a white-collared sea eagle planing with effort-less wing. No doubt he was the island eagle, the married one with his home in the heart of the big creek. I hoped he would have good fishing and wondered idly if I'd be long enough on the island to see his savage brood glaring down from their aerie up in the tree.

Insects lent the air a faint, dreamy humming; the quaint birds in the dwarf trees of the Mound chattered in occasional gossip; the sea was softly crooning on the reef. Anything could be happening to the far-away world; it could not matter to anything here. Curious to realize that all civiliza-tion could come to one crashing end and it would not make the slightest difference to any place like this. Perhaps something like that may happen one day and the world will have to. start all over again, be built up afresh by isolated men left on isolated spots like these. And in thousands of years there would again be tribes of people everywhere. And in thousands again, nations. And the wise men would ponder and declare how the first men appeared on earth, and where they migrated from to people the earth, and why some nations were white, and brown, others red, and yellow, and black. And why they all spoke different languages. But, if such a catastrophe happened to present-day humanity, then how many millions of years would go by before this civilization was all built up again?

In quaint dream thoughts the afternoon wore softly away. But sleep did not quite come. Instinct, the primitive wariness that awakes so soon in a man when living in primitive conditions, fought it.

Towards sundown the cranes in the big mud hole took to heavy-winged flight, hoarsely trumpeting. I peered down at the darkening mangroves.

There was silence for a long time. The sun, rapidly sinking, made the glistening mud surface glow a soft crimson and threw upon it fantastic shadows of branches. Then a grim, wild figure stepped out from the twisted roots and glared up at the Mound. Bending double, he essayed a quick run across the pool and instantly was floundering, struggling madly to recover. He jerked up one leg glued thickly with blue mud, but the other foot had sunk and was so tightly gripped that he had to thrust down his other and strain to drag the foot out. He managed it and turned about to leap back for the mangroves, but his first foot was again deep down hardly inches farther ahead. Violently he strained forward, but both feet were now glued down. He was sinking as I sprang down the Mound to try to throw him a stick. He was caught like a fly in a treacle pot. He leant well forward, with clawing hands levering to draw out a leg. He succeeded, but mud clung heavily to that leg as on one knee he strained to pull out the other. Managing it, he clawed himself flat; then slowly worked his way back while lying flat on the mud. It was a desperate struggle, for his body sank slowly while he could get but sticky leverage for hands and toes and feet; he dared not press those limbs down into the mud again. He was struggling ahead by inches. Presently his outflung arm grasped the leaves of an overhanging branch. Quietly gathering the leaves in his hand until it closed around a twig, he gently pulled on the twig. Two fingers caught the bending branch, then he got a grip; cautiously he worked his hand along as the branch bent towards him.

Pulling slowly, he thrust back the mud with the other arm from the sides of his chest and waist. Thus he crawled forward a few more inches, slung up his other hand, grasped the limb and slowly pulled himself to the roots. His long arms grasped them.

That was intense relief for both of us because this mud hole was far too wide and long for me to have run around it and helped him had he gone under suddenly. The sun was down and he was a shadow clutching the roots, slowly gasping in his breath. I yelled across to hurry. Already the first snaky arms of the tide were creeping up the mud flat. He crawled up the roots with the tide gurgling in, ignoring my shouted warnings. But he was safe now, though he seemed to have collapsed on the roots. He was visible only as a shadowy smudge on the darkening roots. When the foam-bubbling water swirled up to him, he wearily rose and staggered over the water-washed roots to the open reef. He must have had a harder struggle even than appeared, or else received a greater shock.

I ran up on to the Mound and gazed back along the reef. Charlie was just visible wading back towards his camp, the water now almost to his knees. He was quite safe but I did not envy him his walk in the dark along that coral road on which waves were breaking. Charlie's sleep would be fretful this night. I understood now why the cunning old cranes so religiously avoided that particular spot in the mud hole.

Coquet was blinking, her little light flashing across the channel. I gazed a while. Coquet was a sheet-anchor. Even if no vessel came to the island, still the day must come when a lighthouse steamer would arrive to replenish Coquet's oil. One only had to hang on until Coquet wanted oil. All the heart-burnings in the world would not make that day come one whit faster.

I slipped below into the den to brighten up the fire and put on another billy of potatoes. That must have been the reason for Charlie's latest hostility—when he went to the garden and found I'd taken some of the potatoes.

Several days later I strolled across and had a yarn with Charlie. He had quite recovered, but was morose. We made no mention of the affair of the mud hole. He brightened up a bit as we yarned and presently pulled out a tin specimen from under his bunk. He had found it half way up the Peak.

"What do you think of that?" he inquired.

"It is a rich little specimen," I said.

"Yes. I found it half way up the Peak. There's a rich lode there somewhere."

"I wouldn't be sure, Charlie," I replied doubtfully. "The island is far too small to hold anything but leaders."

"There's a rich reef here somewhere," he replied doggedly, "and I'm going to carry on digging at the Peak until I find it."

"I wish you luck, but so far as I'm concerned I've had enough of tin and wolfram on this island. All I want is to get away from it."

He shook his head in turn.

"There's not one chance in a thousand of a vessel calling here. Waste of time to think about it."

"But what about the ketch? She goes at least one trip every three months from Cooktown to Port Stewart, the wet season excepted. Even if it is difficult to land here there must come a time when the weather will be calm when she passes."

"She thinks we've been picked up long ago."

"I cannot see your reasoning."

But he only shrugged. It was not till long afterwards that I learnt of his instructions to the skipper. Charlie lived in an entirely different world to mine. He did not want his fellow men, whereas I longed for my old mate Dick and our packhorses and our happy trips on the mainland, with the good days among the boys at the mining camps. But Charlie was a hermit; had been a recluse for years and years.

That night while lying on the Mound I fell asleep from gazing up at the stars. Suddenly I awoke, for the night was filled with a quickly increasing musical throbbing. All was halcyon calm, a night on' which an insect could sing loudly. Gliding through the velvet gloom was a throbbing tower of starry lights.

I gazed longingly at that fairy picture. Through the intense stillness could be plainly felt the vibration of the big ship's engines. A China boat, going south! She seemed to be gliding over a sea of polished velvet, her lights water-reflected under a starlit sky. And so utterly close!

In a frenzy I lit a fire, scraping leaves and grass—anything I could snatch to make a flame, then stood in red outline against the blackness.

In vain, of course. Even if they gave a second thought to it they would think it a natives' fire, would believe it lit by a canoe load of natives who had come out fishing from the mainland. Why couldn't it be so in fact? Why couldn't the wretched natives come while I was here? Those steamer people would think it only a fire from some *beche-de-mer* camp, a landing party of the luggers sometimes seen out on the Great Barrier Reef not far away. They would believe it anything except what it really was.

The big ship kept serenely on, gliding close to the island through the deep channel. Calm weather and the deep water of a big tide were probably tempting her skipper to take a short cut. As she passed I could plainly see one side of her decking under the electric lights reflected upon the clean white paint. The great live sea itself seemed to be breathlessly listening to the fairy piano music that apparently came floating down from the sky. And a woman's voice singing!

The vessel passed. With the lessening hum of her engines the brilliant lights grew smaller and smaller until she was but a jewelled firefly gliding over a sea of velvet dreams.

She left behind her a crushing' sense of loneliness. All that I was missing while marooned on this wretched island seemed to come in a rush of longing and memories. I had been so cheerful after those feeds of potatoes, then this vessel had come swiftly in the night and as swiftly throbbed away.

The tide came in still farther, almost silently, only a gentle murmuring and whispering as of waters very gently spilling over the rim of a mighty basin. Several hours drifted by.

A star gleamed and vanished low down right upon the water. Without interest I noticed it. Presently it gleamed again, to vanish like Coquet in miniature. That instant recognition of Coquet made me spring up. Presently, the star flashed, nearer now, flashed right upon the water—and vanished. Realization came instantly. The tides and currents had carried it here. Would it land? Hardly, because the tide was now on the turn. Excited, I stared down at the dark channel. The tiny star appeared again, blinking just above the water, its brave little light clearly visible, just as it would be visible to a lookout up on a masthead. Blinking and vanishing, blinking and vanishing, it came gliding along with the tide . . . hesitated . . . then came straight in towards the reef. Alas, a current stronger than the tide caught it and swept it along the channel again. Gliding past the Mound, its recurrent flash was visible for a long time until at last it disappeared around the island. If only I had had a boat!

Under that tiny star was opium, a large tin or sealed canister of it. Almost certainly it had been thrown overboard from that passing steamer. When it struck the water it floated away as a buoy, its clockwork set ticking. Five minutes later and its light would flash. It would continue to flash until picked up by a waiting lugger.

Apparently there had been no waiting lugger. These last few days of dead calm had prevented it from being on time at the rendezvous. Now the little vessel with its load of dreams was floating away at the mercy of tide and current.

20

The Opium

Next morning brought a cheerless breakfast on the remains of last night's fish and potatoes. Yet, everything was the same; the island and everything on it, the sky and the sea. Another day had come with the same sun and life and hope. All should have been as cheery as yesterday. The passing of a steamer in the night had made the whole world miserable—my world.

The tide came lapping over the reef with hardly a ripple. And on it something came floating gently in. I had not noticed it, being wretchedly occupied in being miserable. That floating thing looked like a piece of seaweed, some floating weed had caught upon it. Suddenly I remembered last night and hurried down to the water's edge. The flotsam came nearer. It bore the tiniest of mastheads upon which was furled a wee flag. If there had been the faintest breeze that flag, would have been bravely fluttering. It was the opium tin, brought back by the returning tide.

I waded out, tingling with curiosity though wary of sharks. The tin came drifting sluggishly closer with a decided list to port. At last I grasped it. A watertight kerosene tin it appeared to be at first sight. But it was actually larger, supporting a clever "topmast" of wire built just like those steel trellis-masts on some American battleships. This mast rose two feet above the tin and right at the top was the neat little flash lamp. Something had gone wrong with the mechanism for the lamp was out, or else the clockwork was regulated so cleverly that the light would flash only at night. Above the mast projected a tiny wooden flagpole. That tiny flag on a calm sea would be visible quite a distance to a man with glasses searching for it from the masthead of a lugger. Sitting on the reef I admired the thing, delaying to break it open. No doubt as to what was inside, for it was known in Cooktown and farther south in Cairns that opium was constantly thrown overboard that way, from China boats steaming down the coast. I thought of Charlie, and glanced along the reef. The tide was coming in, but it was still possible to splash along the reef right to his camp. I hurried. This was too great a treat to keep from Charlie. We would spend days gloating over this visitation; it would supply an entire change in conversation, a new mutual interest. If only he was not in one of his bad moods.

Nearly so. He was sitting morosely by the fire.

"What do you think of this?" I shouted.

He stared, then his face showed interest; he reached out for the tin.

"Where did you get it?" he growled pleasantly.

"It came floating in with the tide."

"Must have been thrown overboard from that China boat last night."

"That's what I thought. Did you see the steamer?"

"No, I heard her engines. How shrewd these chaps are! See how cleverly this is built. That signal flag of yours!"

He glanced up sharply.

"What about it?"

"Pull it down!" He stood up, his face eager, his eyes fairly dancing.

"Why pull it down?"

"Don't you understand? This calm has delayed some lugger from being on time to pick up the tin! No doubt she should have been lying off Coquet last night. She can't be far away! She'll see your flag and search the 4 island."

"Then she'll pick us up! Thank heaven! I had not thought of that!"

"Pick us up be damned. Do you imagine opium smugglers would pick us up? They are more likely to give us a bullet for interfering in their business.

See this!"

He ripped the tomahawk into the tin and split it open, disclosing tight-packed tins inside. "See!" he pointed triumphantly. He ripped a side from the container and poured out the tins, one hundred and forty-four of them.

"There you are. When we left Cooktown a tin of this brand was worth £20 anywhere in Chinatown. That's £2880 worth of opium lying there. Do you think a crew of Asiatics are going to let us get away with that?"

I stared at him.

"Pull down the flag," he almost entreated. "All they will want is their opium; the last thing in the world they would do would be to take us off this island if we gave them back their opium. Don't you realize they'd know we would put the show away when they landed us at Cooktown? And that the Customs men would be hiding off Coquet waiting for them the very next time a China boat was due to pass by. The smugglers would be forced to find a new rendezvous; it would put their organization all out of plumb. If they find out we've got this opium their object will be to silence us, not ' to take us off and let us advertise their plant."

"But this is Australia," I protested. "They daren't do anything to us! If they were uneasy about landing us at Cooktown they'd simply take us off and land us anywhere on the mainland and be only too glad that they'd recovered their opium."

"Australia be damned. This is a lonely island on one of the loneliest coastlines in the world. Who sails these waters? A very occasional steamer going to China or Darwin. Who else? Quite a lot of pearling luggers and *beche-de-mer* cutters manned by Asiatics. No one else. This is their coast while they sail it. To them we are two unknown white foreigners entirely cut off from the world, and we've not only taken possession of nearly £3000 worth of their opium, but we've spoilt the secrecy of their receiving base. And we're in a position to put them away to the Customs officials down south. Bah! They'll shut our mouths once for all. We'll never leave the island—unless it's with a stone around our necks over the edge of the reef. Pull down that flag before it is too late!"

He was a different Charlie, years had dropped from him. And he meant every eager word he said.

"All right!" I agreed, and started running back along the track to pull down the signal pole.

"Bank your fire so that no smoke can show," yelled Charlie. "And don't leave anything lying about!"

There was nothing much to leave lying about, the camp of an aboriginal could hardly have been more primitive. When I Returned to Charlie we climbed stealthily up the Peak, he taking the lead eager as a schoolboy. I hardly knew the man.

There was no sail in sight. Eagerly we scanned the sea all around.

"No sign of her!" I said in disappointment.

"Don't be too sure. Don't show yourself on the skyline; you'd look like a beacon to a vessel out there. She may be lying behind Coquet, or she may be close to the mangroves away behind our island. We wouldn't see her there while she kept in close to the trees."

Charlie was all on the gaze, eager to talk. We debated the pros and cons for quite a while, then suddenly Charlie exclaimed:

"Look! Here she conies! Keep down out of sight."

I gazed around where his hand pointed, then crouched low. Around the shore edge of the Peak away below a dinghy appeared, the coloured crew straining at the oars. Then another and another, pulling hard as they slowly towed a rakish looking *beche-de-mer* cutter, black painted. A speedy looking little vessel. A Japanese steered her, several men stood at bow and stern while one at the masthead was examining the calm waters through field glasses.

"Don't show yourself," cautioned Charlie. "They'll concentrate on the shoreline but they might glance up here now and again. On a bright day like this, they'd spot the top of your head against the skyline."

Above all things in the world that was the very thing I had wished these months past. I lay there wondering at Charlie, wondering at myself for not standing erect and yelling. If we gave them their own opium it seemed a cheap price to pay for a passage back to civilization. But Charlie's reasoning seemed grimly sound. "Dead men tell no tales" did not appear melodramatic under the circumstances. Those men down there were engaged in illegal smuggling for big prizes. They were aliens who put quite a different price on morals and life, especially foreign life. If we walked to the shore and gave them the opium they could easily take us aboard, learn our story, then drop us overboard any night. If they didn't, they would not dare to meet steamers here again, all their system would be disorganized, they would have to advise headquarters in Hong Kong or Shanghai and reorganize their system entirely. And the "heads" would not relish the trouble and danger and expense of that. The longer I thought of it the more Charlie's reasoning rang true.

"They'll be angry men," said Charlie. "They only missed that China boat by hours. And now they've lost over £2000 worth of opium. All for the need of a puff of wind. Their skipper will get caned over the knuckles for this."

"And the crew will lose their prize money." "Yes, and be mad about it, too."

"It's a wonder we have not noticed the black cutter before. Is Coquet light their regular rendezvous I wonder?"

"They'd lie in behind Cape Melville by day, and sail for Coquet by dark. They'd pick up the tin and be away in the dark before dawn. No stray pearling vessels would notice them hanging about then."

"I suppose they get rid of the stuff through Cooktown or Cairns."

"Yes/ simple. Sail into Cooktown with a cargo of *beche-de-mer,* sell it to the Chinese merchants and sell the opium at the same time. Or make their selling port farther south at Cairns or Townsville. They've got legitimate business in all three ports. Sometimes they don't sail into the port with the stuff, but approach by night, then sail into the coast at an agreed-on spot where an agent is waiting. They land the stuff and he takes it overland in perfect safety. They stand off shore then sail into port in daytime and all the Customs officers in the world could search their boat and not find a solitary tin of opium."

"By Jove!"

"What?"

"They *must* know we're here! They *must* have seen the signal flag—it's visible miles out to sea!"

"Out to sea, yes!" chuckled Charlie, "but not close up against the mangroves away around the island. They've drifted all night, have been pulling for hours maybe, hugging the mangrove edge all the closer towards dawn. They'd take no more risk than they had to. They came from around behind the Hill remember, and we had that flag down soon after dawn. No, if they had seen it they'd have landed here already."

Slowly the black cutter neared Coquet Island. The anchor splashed down, the chain rattled musically across the water. The lookout man remained at the masthead while other Japanese took command of the dinghies which scattered, rowing closely around the shore.

"They'll examine every yard of the shore around Coquet," said Charlie, "then come here and row along the reef and around the island. They won't see my camp for it is sheltered not only by mangroves but by the lagoon and reef; they'll keep to the reef edge and won't come within hundreds of yards of the camp. The Mound will have no attraction for them; it's only the shoreline they'll be interested in. Sure you've left nothing lying about, no crab shells or fish bones down near the reef?"

"Nothing. And there are no tracks because the tide washes them out. The only tracks are at the well which they can't see. They'd see your track from the camp to the well if they came inland."

"They won't do that," said Charlie—"not unless they're short of water and happen to know of the well, which isn't likely. If so, and they search inland, we must take to the mangroves."

"Why? We could easily bluff it out. They don't know that we have found the opium!" "Then why are we hiding here?"

I glanced at Charlie, then across at the cutter. Of course they would know. If we knew nothing of the opium we should have been standing plainly on the Peak long ago. Two lonely men on a barren island do not let such a chance of a talk and fresh stores go by unless they have some good reason for doing so. I realized that this exciting interlude might possibly lead to unpleasant adventure. How shrewd Charlie was! And what a different man!

"If they forced us to take to the mangroves," I said slowly, "we'd be in desperate plight. They'd only have to camp by the Hill, the Peak, and the Mound. The tide must drive us out of the mangroves. What then?"

"They'd have to split up their small forces and post them in three places: several at the

Hill, several at the Peak, several at the Mound. And three men, at least, would have to stay aboard the cutter. Where would the men be to catch us when and if we came from the mangroves? Two spare men at the very most. Well, we are two men. Besides, we know the mangroves; they don't. They would be like fish out of water. And how would those two men know where to wait for us? We would have all the cover; they would have none. We could come out of the mangroves wherever we liked, so long as it was on the Hill or Peak side. Then again, if they posted two men to watch the Mound we could come out of the mangroves anywhere around the Mound and tackle them by surprise."

"Water?"

"How did you ensure your water supply though so far from the well?"

Ah, how indeed!

"Then we'd have our spears to get us food, and we'd carry firesticks," added Charlie.

"H'm. If it does work out that way, we're in for an interesting time."

"We are. You've wanted something to break the monotony; now you've got it—or will have, if they discover there are two white men on this island."

Perhaps it was this same change in the mono-tony, with its chance of lively times to come, that had so changed Charlie. No one could have wished for a better mate when he was like this. I felt the reaction too, while peering out across the channel at that black cutter, almost wishing that they would discover our presence and investigate.

"If they do come," I said eagerly, "they must row ashore in a dinghy. If they chased us about the island they would not have nearly enough men to watch the Peak, the Hill, the Mound, the mangroves, the cutter, and the dinghy. They'd certainly leave it unguarded. If our position became desperate we could sneak on the dinghy at night, row across to the cutter and try to seize her. That's the last thing they .would expect."

"Why shouldn't' we seize her?" growled Charlie. "We'd be masters of the situation then. We could sail the vessel away and keep her or sell her. They daren't say a word. They couldn't anyway; we'd be away and they'd be here."

I whistled. Charlie somehow took my breath away.

21

Charlie's Thoughts

But circumstances did not turn us into pirates, nor were we compelled to play hide-and-seek with the smugglers. Unaware of our presence, the three dinghies eventually rowed across the channel and began slowly cruising along the reef. One Japanese waded ashore and searched carefully along the mangrove edge towards the Mound, even among the twisted roots at the mouths of several of the larger inlets.

Had the opium tin gone sailing up there they would never have found it; it would have voyaged into the heart of the mangroves and become caught amongst the roots and trunks. But these seamen did not know how the tides rushed along the creeks into the heart of the labyrinth. They would search no farther than the edge.

I wondered if ambergris, the treasure Charlie was always searching for, had ever been washed in a big lump away into the heart of the forest. If so, it would be lying there in the slimy mud. the burrows of sea grubs and crawly things around it. Thousands of pounds worth could lie there, and instead of making a lovely scent for a lady's perfume, it would lie in the mud until at last it rotted away. And so the opium would have perished had it been washed away into those creeks. Not that the beastly stuff was worth anything to us. It was hard indeed. What great numbers of Chinese would give their souls to smoke was worthless to us. And yet we were dying for a smoke.

In late afternoon the smugglers disappeared around the island; it would take them far longer to search these shores than little Coquet. Charlie lived every moment of those days and nights. He was continually doing "sentry go," hardly letting me out of his sight. It was easily one of the best weeks we had had on the island. For a week, every day, we got a glimpse of the black cutter as her dinghies searched the entire Howick Group, testing every place where erratic currents and tides might have washed the opium on to island or mud bank. Finally, one glorious sunset, she filled her sails and headed south, a little black vessel sailing into red to fade slowly in pink and vanish into the gloaming.

"She's gone!" sighed Charlie.

"Yes. What now?"

"Carry on, of course."

Carry on! Those words held very different meanings for me and for Charlie. Gazing towards where the lugger had vanished in the crimson west, I wondered if I had not been an utter fool after all. But no, Charlie's reasoning had been quite sound. Those men were aliens and desperate; Charlie and I were two lonely white men. And now life promised to be much more bearable. We were good friends, and not nearly so bread hungry.

The potatoes had allayed to a considerable extent the craving for bread. Charlie was again the best of companions. If he only remained so, if we both remained so, life would be bearable until we were picked up. He even invited me to shift my camp back to his. That offer was very, very tempting, but memory of his chronic turns induced a half-hearted excuse. It would spoil everything if we camped together, when he went sick and crazy again. Whereas if we camped apart we could avoid one another when he took a turn, but meet, and be good friends on the good days. I had quite given up wondering how he managed to survive that awful trouble. He so very definitely looked on it as his own business anyway.

Time slipped by pleasantly. Occasionally we went fishing together. We would go along the reef around his side of the island, and his eyes seldom wandered from the reef edge whenever we were away from the mangroves.

"Still looking for ambergris?"

"Yes. And never found any. All I've picked up so far have been hardened lumps of fat thrown overboard from some vessel goodness knows where. Those lumps of fat have drifted here, and have pulled my leg a dozen times. But I'll find the real ambergris yet."

"It would have to be a big lump to be worth what that opium would be worth to the smugglers."

"Yes. Lumps far larger than that have been found though. But fancy you finding that opium!"

"If it had only been a case of tinned meats it would have been a godsend to us. We don't smoke opium. It's like what a nugget of gold would be to a man perishing for a drink in the desert. The irony of it almost makes me cry. Now, just imagine how we would have yelled with delight if that big tin had only held tins of tobacco! I'd do almost anything for a smoke now."

"In these places a man has to take what the sea gives him," replied Charlie soberly, "and be thankful. We've managed to live here for months after the last of our civilized tucker gave out—lived quite comfortably with little exertion. Many shipwrecked people have perished under far easier conditions, more still have perished in circumstances similar to ours. If only we had a dinghy we could cruise from island to island and across to the mainland when we wanted to. We could make this our base. Time is our own; we've no responsibilities; we are our own masters. Very few men in all the world can say that."

But policy warned me against being drawn into a discussion when our views were so entirely opposite. This life was apparently Charlie's ideal; the wonder was why he had chosen this barren hole instead of some much more favoured island. But if he had chosen elsewhere the island would probably have been occupied, either by whites or coloured people. The fact was Charlie was a prospector; his life was lived in the wild places in an insatiable quest for gold or minerals. He had believed that this island contained tin. That decided him. The search for it would occupy his time and thought. With the mineral won he could buy things through passing

135

boats, and so develop his island home; buy tools, put up a comfortable hut, plant other vegetables and fruit- trees, even run fowls and goats on this tiny place. Buy a dinghy and whatever other simple necessities he required, lay in a stock of chemicals to treat his wound. And thereafter be absolutely independent of the world, his own master in every respect for the remainder of his life.

For recreation and other food he could fish with spear and line, could wander the great reef in company with the gulls. The sea eagles and the gulls and he would be foraging in company, their combined interest the sea. He would seek for whatever the waves might cast up, wreckage or ambergris or other flotsam. His would be much more interesting than an ordinary beachcomber's life; he would have his mine as well as the sea's gifts; his goats and fowls and garden, and dinghy to go cruising on exploratory voyages, with the island always as base. He could put up a sail and prospect the mainland coastline for mineral; on other trips he could cruise from island to island, seeking mineral, meeting other white wanderers and different natives, living different scenes from week to week, month by month. When tired of wandering he could return here to his garden and fowls and goats, until the urge came to sail again. And this island home was so small and isolated that no one would ever desire to take it from him.

Easy to understand now why he had so readily agreed about seizing the black cutter— had encouraged the possible seizing of it; why he had, day by day, gazed so longingly at those dinghies. What a happy position he would have been in had we successfully seized the cutter! He could have sailed to Cooktown for his own stores, could have transported his own mineral or pearl-shell or other gleanings to civilization when and how he wished. Easy to understand now why night after night he had discussed the seizing of the cutter should any one of a number of eventualities arise, the careful plans he had evolved, should such and such an event arise. Had we actually seized that cutter, then, after the rightful owners had rowed away in the dinghies, Charlie could have returned, could have sailed the cutter at the big high tides over the reef and into the lagoon, even right on into the mouth of the big creek. She could never, never have been seen from there. He would have been king not only of his own island, but of his own ship.

Obviously Charlie had come here with his own dreams. Why he had brought another man with him to this forlorn place was hard to imagine. He surely must have realized that not another man in a hundred thousand would wish to live his life here. On a tropic isle rich with coco-nut palms and bananas and tropical fruits and vegetables, with plenty of running water and other enticements, yes. Perhaps he wanted to find out first just whether he could live all alone with that wound of his, and far from any help. Once certain he could do so, he probably thought he would get rid of his companion by helping him aboard any passing lugger.

I wondered whether he would not be afraid of his own thoughts. What effect would this life have on a solitary man, after months had gone by? A determined man like Charlie might go to bed at sunset, train himself to fall straight asleep, and awake at sunrise. But even with his mind diverted by the interests of the day, he must think sometimes. Often I had found it hard enough after the fishing was done just to sit up on the Lookout and gaze out to sea and think and think and think, or not think and think and think. How a man could voluntarily resign himself to that sort of thing for life was a puzzle.

That night we yarned by Charlie's fire. He was in high good humour, had been so ever since the opium came ashore. In the circumstances it was quite worthless, yet it's coming had made all the difference to two men on an island. We had not been such mates since our first month on the wretched place.

"What do you think of at nights?" I ventured. "Anything, or just nothing at all."

"Depends on what humour I'm in. That has nothing to do with Me. If it had, I'd always be the pleasantest company imaginable to myself. When something steals over me, my thoughts are black as hell. When everything is all right, I'm too cheerful to think much: I whistle. If the humour is intermediate, I think of all sorts of things ; how to do things, how to improve the conditions of the world, how to cure disease, how to build things; where we come from and where we go—and why. Lots of nights I only think of the island, how to build it up out of a wilderness of mangroves and mud and turn it into a wonderful home. Some nights I think of the mainland and the blacks I know out in the ranges, and where mineral might be out in the gorges and around the Musgraves. Sometimes I think of the fish. Wonder what fish there are down at the bottom of the corals; what size the gropers are down there; whether there are any real sea serpents; what a man would see if he could only sink to the bottom of the ocean and walk about as naturally as the fish swim. Sometimes I think about the stars. It all depends on the humours; they regulate my thoughts." "You mean that your thoughts are regulated by your state of health?"

"Not exactly, though that has a lot to do with it in another way. Bad health, whenever I feel it, clouds all thoughts. What I mean is the humours. I might be as right as pie, but humours might sway me quite against my will. My thoughts are all right. They'd be good enough friends to me, only I can't regulate them at will except on certain days. I try to steer my thoughts straight as a steersman tries to steer a sailing ship. But the humours bring all sorts of influences to bear, just as the wind bears in varying degrees on a sailing ship. Every man is the same, I reckon. Otherwise, every man would steer straight to a certain goal just as a mechanical steamer steers straight to a certain port. Each one of us when a schoolboy would decide what his life was to be and would go straight for it, never varying a hairbreadth. We'd all be mechanical then. But Nature has made us like a sailing vessel and then planked us straight down on a sea of life with a mind as the rudder, but humours as the wind."

"H'm. Then to your way of thinking Man cannot rigidly control his life."

"Of course he can't. Man isn't man; he's a dozen things planted in a flesh framework that he doesn't understand. I'm only responsible in degree for my actions and thoughts. So are you; so is every one."

"Do you ever wonder what happens when we die?"

"Sometimes. Can't help it. Lived so long among the blacks. They discuss that subject often—but not like we do. They're sure. They are certain we live again. I think so too, but not because of their reasoning. I *feel* it. These humours as I call them, and this Me that is in me let me feel in vague ways now and then that the Me in this hide of mine is only there for the time being. When I die, this bag of bones drops to dust—and a damned good job too! The sooner the better. But the Me that was the life in it, will keep on living. Don't ask in what way: I don't know, and don't care. I'm just certain, that's all. I'm certain, too, that these humours, as I call them, won't have such an influence on me after death. I'll be able to control the Me much more easily then; won't have this damned cumbersome body to lug about with all the worries of bad health and a hundred other things that keep a man' chained like an animal to a cart."

We were silent for quite a time. Charlie, even in the good days of the first month, had never spoken like this.

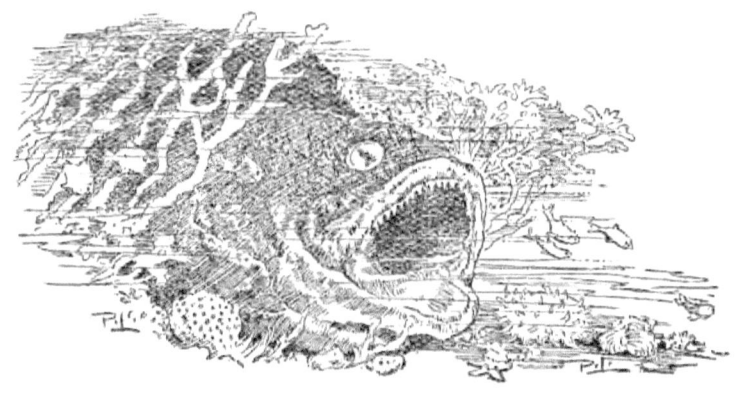

22

Mysteries of the Sea

During the long days when the tide was out and the fishing done I'd often go for a walk along the reef away towards the "back" of the island. There a man could walk quite a long distance with the sunlit sea to the left, and never-ending mangroves to the right. The reef was a great broad road of white and grey, ramparts of a mighty encircling wall that held back the sea. But for that wall built up from the ocean bed by tiny coral polyps there would have been no island. The reef held countless fairy palaces of amazing beauty enlivened by fascinating life.

As the weeks had dragged into months, I learnt that this reef held secrets of life stretching back possibly to the Beginning. There were water things living here that were partly land things too; animal and fish and plant life in amazing stages of development and beauty and ugliness, but each having the keenest efficiency in its own sphere. Things that ate with teeth, and by suction, by inhaling, by crushing, by boring. Things that sucked in sand and passed it right through them, retaining only the minute insect or vegetable life living in the sand; things, both plant and fish and degrees in between, that sucked in the water only to strain it of the life brought by the tides; things that lived by ways impossible to fathom. Big things like the moving life contained in the branching corals and the giant anemones and giant clams interested me first of all because they were so obvious. The beautiful growths that came out of the corals were always pulsing and moving, receding and coming and spreading; the big anemones were continually spreading out to let tiny fish peep forth, only to close them in again; the waterspouts of the clams were continual^ squirting; numerous things were click, click, clicking, battalions of little crabs were slithering, with a rattling of shells as a man walked by.

Experience taught that it was not altogether vibration from strange feet that caused the clams to shut their shells; it was mainly to eject used up water. They lay with their shells open, exposing softly coloured flesh of emerald green or variegated browns and heliotropes. And through this soft mantle were two holes like fleshy tunnels. The animal inside would take water through one hole, absorb the food the water contained and, closing its shell, squirt the water from the other hole. Then the shell would slowly open again. I used to creep silently on these shells and watch them eating and pulsing, gorging and closing. Some were immense, especially those that grew just over the edge of the reef down where the deep water began. Bedded down there in a coral hole camouflaged by waving seaweeds, one great fellow was certainly five feet long, and as broad. His shell, cleared of growing seaweeds and of other shells, would weigh hundredweights. The soft fleshy mantle he draped over the lip of his shell was marvellously beautiful when visible during those hours that the sun's rays shone straight down through the water. The strength of the great muscle that could clap tight that mighty shell must have been truly gigantic. I shuddered at the thought of a swimmer accidentally placing arm or foot in that great maw. Probably, no man would, for this fellow was plain to see. But there were others so draped by seaweeds that it was very difficult to detect them. A swimmer diving down would, of course, not see them.

Many coral pools on the exposed surface of the reef were fascinating—the shallow water like a mirror, its every form of life magnified by sunlight. Even if a man returned to the same pool day after day, he could still discover something he had missed before. The grottoed sides of the pool lined with stag-horn corals and the delicate coral fernery of blended reds and mauves, rose-pinks and blues and browns and whites mantled the pool in soft amazing beauty. Rivalling them and even more fascinating were the animal flowers, coral and anemone rosettes and chrysanthemums. One big golden velvet pansy with crimson spots suddenly became a fish and swam away.

Several corals reminded me irresistibly of glowing fungoids in the depths of the Daintree Jungle. Among them spread the russet-golden tresses of sea-maids' hair with pulsing things of vegetable growth that quivered and opened and closed with arms and wings, mouths and bodies suggesting the fluffy things that line the necks of women's evening shawls. Only these things were softer and more beautiful. On the bottom over clean white sand a scarlet crab would sidle, perhaps a vivid blue one.

And among it all, diving in and out of the delicate coral branches, in and out of the mouths of anemones, and flashing across the pool were the tiniest, most brilliant and cheekiest of fish. Their colour schemes though bizarre suited them amazingly. Some wore large, brilliant spots; others vivid bars of scarlet and black. Some were bright blue, others red; some were orange-coloured, strikingly splashed with bands of black. All had the tiniest of brilliant eyes, the cheekiest of fairy tails, an amazing air of the liveliest vivacity. Most had the sharpest of little fish faces, others were snouted like jewelled pigs, still others had bulging eyes. But each had a quaint individuality. All could disappear like a flash into the corals or sea plants. After a while their tiny heads would reappear here, there, and everywhere, living jewels peeping from a great live sponge. Then an adventurous one would dart into the pool and gaze inquisitively around; several would follow, and in a moment the pool would become alive again. They appeared to take a keen interest in the man-thing gazing down at them.

Occasionally there would be an ogre at the bottom of such a pool, hard to see at first for he lay motionless, his colours merging with the sand and coral and plants. A striped and mottled carpet shark, this fellow.

Living in that same pool was another demon, a small octopus that could change into varying colours as you gazed. No matter where his creepy tentacles crawled they changed to the colour of what they touched, whether plant or coral or sand. Wherever he was, he appeared part of what he was crouching upon. One day two of his tentacles were reddish like the reddish *beche-de-mer* across which they were flung, the others were the brown of the brown coral plant they gripped. His body was the white of the sand. A little fish swam over him and a tentacle instantly coiled around it. The horrible body changed colours as it moved into a crevice to enjoy its meal.

One long pool, for some reason, was always a favourite haunt of needle-spined sea-urchins whose long black spines were constantly moving. Those clusters of black needles seemed the last place in the world for a sanctuary, but there was a wee brown fish who would always flee to them when I dropped a coral stone into the pool. Here, too, crawled the black *beche-de-mer* like a wrinkled German sausage, nosing the sand as the feelers about its queer mouth scooped the sand into its queer insides.

In this pool I played hide-and-seek for a long time with a quaint fish. A big black eye would stare up from between the coral branches: it would never move. One day I crept to the pool and saw the fish, a tiny thing with a vivid black spot on his body. Whether he and his kind let this "eye" peep from the corals to scare off other fish one cannot say, but its menace certainly is a striking camouflage.

Here, too, I made a great discovery while watching a ball of gorgeous seaweed slowly edging across the bottom of the pool. Seaweeds occasionally move in the queerest of ways, but this weed was actually walking. It shuddered violently when I speared it. The weed really was living and growing, but a quaint crab was making it walk. He was covered with long, strong hairs and with these he had fastened the tufts of plant to himself; the hairs gripped the tendrils just as the tendrils of passion-flowers will twist upon themselves. Tiny roots of these weeds had actually grown into the joints of the crab's shell. He must have an uncomfortable time when forced to discard the old shell and grow a new one, timidly searching among the corals for just the right type of weed, carefully pruning off little pieces with his claws, painfully reaching over his back and placing them where the hairs could wind around them. I wondered how long it took him to do the job, how long it took for the hairs to twist so tightly around the plants, how long before the vegetable camouflage took root. Perhaps some of the tiny pieces died and then the poor old crab would have to remove them, unwind his hairs and find a new weed and transplant it. When his growing garden reached full bloom he was safely camouflaged from enemies so long as he "froze" quite still. But life must be hard work for him, carrying that garden about on his back.

In those pools, provided he was not moping about and wishing he would be rescued, a man could find things to keep his interest alive. To a stranger, at first sight the reef might be disappointing. Its surface was one huge expanse of grey and white, all dead coral. For coral dies when it builds up to the air. But in every pool and over the edge of the reef was a fairyland of riotous life. When the tide was out I would lie on the edge of the reef and, with my eyes just touching the water surface, stare straight down.

It was fascinating staring down a wall through sunlit water into a gloomy shadow world far below. Among vast coral gardens glided fish of all sizes. Those lively ones of brilliant colours were entrancing to watch; some streaked past like living gold, their fantails shimmering with movement. But others glided by like sinister grey shadows. Sea plants waved tendrils that might have been the tentacles of an old man octopus. Squids, evil-looking brutes, shot through the gloom. Fair'-things, some with drooping tassels lit with phosphoric light, floated like gigantic bubbles into the gloom of subterranean cliffs. Here and there were gloomy areas indicating caverns that ran in under the reef, and there at times I would glimpse the shadowy form of a giant groper going or coming. One such cavern was the home of a monster, the terror of the reef. Masses of sea-maids' hair floated before this cavern mouth and just below it was a sea plant like a monstrous staghorn growing to a cliff. The leaves of this animal-plant were continuously folding and unfolding, writhing far out to convulsively come together again. With every sinuous movement it glowed in phosphoric lights of green and red. The groper would float at the mouth of the cavern, his great head gloomily visible among the weeds. When I put my eyes right down into the water I could see his eyes glaring up, magnified till they were saucers of a liquid, glowing green. Now and again he would slowly roll and his cavernous mouth would open as if in a prodigious yawn. At such times his teeth gleamed in rows of ivory. Easy to understand how a naked swimmer, speeding down past such a cavern, had had his arm snapped off by one bite. The local fish avoided that cavern mouth as the plague. But they knew when the monster was away from home. A wild scatter of fish was sure signal that he was returning.

Occasionally a banded sea snake would shoot out from the plants and like lightning coil itself around a passing fish. The desperate struggle ended out of sight among the thrashing sea fronds. Then a big coral eel would speed past, fish darting aside from him. Even so far down in the gloom those big eels looked vicious brutes.

I wished for a roomy bell of glass lit up electrically that could be lowered far down the side of the reef into the deepest gloom. A man sitting in such a bell, with a search-light, could train it on to the cliffy reef and spy within an almost unbelievable world.

The flotsam and jetsam around the island shores held stories too—it was like a breath from the far-away world to see even a board washed up by the tide. It always meant a quickening of the walk, an eager reading of the disconnected words to learn where the board came from. It might be a petrol case, or a board with half an address on it; it might be marked with Japanese or Chinese characters. Anyway, it was a board fresh from the sea and it had recently been in civilization. At the back of the island the reef was indented by tiny bays among the mangroves. This was the weather side and most recent flotsam was washed up here. On turning the Point I would always gaze eagerly along the reef and mangrove edge, alert for case or plank or anything that might have been washed up. Unfortunately it was a long way from the Peak and Mound, and one always had to be ready to hurry back from the tide. It was maddening to think that a *beche-de-mer* cutter could easily be fishing around this back of the island without even being visible from the Mound. Washed up among the mangroves here, to be wedged among the roots, were shell- and slime- encrusted spars and planks, relics of ships that might have gone down hundreds of miles away. It was always with a quickening of the pulse that I found one of these tragic fragments and by the faint, decayed evidence tried to piece the story together. Even if it was only a stick, it had been in the hands of man. At such times loneliness gripped one—just the open sea and the shrieking gulls, the reef and the mangroves, with a man bending over some relic from the sea.

23

The Rescue

One morning I yawned awake, climbed the Mound and stared out to sea. The rising sun was a fiery ball balancing upon the rim of the sea. Soon it would grow steadier but far smaller as it concentrated on its daily job of lighting half the world.

My heart suddenly beat almost painfully. Floating out of the haze around distant Cape Melville was a snow-white mainsail, small as the wing of a gull. But it was a sail, and on that tack and with the wind as it was, it was heading directly towards the island. It was on the Cooktown tack, heading south. I watched with beating heart. There was only the faintest breeze; if it did not strengthen, the vessel would hardly get here by sunset. With a strengthening wind she would try to make Coquet her night anchorage. I felt certain of it: she was on the direct tack.

An hour later and another sail came beating around the Cape, followed by another. All on the same tack.

Pearling luggers; bound for Cooktown to discharge pearl-shell and take in stores. My heavens! What if one of them is painted black!

Instantly I dismissed the absurd thought for the smuggler would not be cruising in company.

Premonition brought immediate action lest sickening uncertainty gain ascendancy. I leapt down into the crevice and snatched together the few ragged possessions. I'd hurry to the Peak, sling the blanket to the bamboo flagpole, then run down and tell Charlie. That blanket flag would be visible for miles, and if the vessels came quite close they must see me, too, signalling beside it. If only they came to anchor as close as Coquet, they could not fail to see a man signalling from the Peak just across on Howick Island.

The tide was still going out as I splashed along the reef in wild delight. This thing *must* be really true. Yes! From half way up the Peak those three tiny sails were plainly visible, heading this way. This was their tack for a certainty. But unless the wind freshened it would be night before they could arrive here. The tide would soon be right out; Charlie would go fishing. The flagpole could wait. I ran down the Peak to Charlie's camp.

He was just banking up his fire, his fish spear nearby. He was a bundle of rags, his hair had grown prodigiously, his beard was a fright.

"Charlie! Charlie! Boats are coming. Three of them. They're tacking straight for the island!"

He straightened up and stared from bloodshot eyes; he was morose again.

"Which way are they coming?" he growled.

"Around Cape Melville. South. Three of them in line. Pearling luggers. There's hardly any wind, but they're tacking direct this way. They'll make Coquet a night anchorage I'm certain."

"No need to get excited. They're not here yet."

"No, but they *will* be. I've rolled up my swag and taken it to the Peak. I'm going to build up that cairn of rocks and plant that flag as high as it can possibly go."

"If they can't see it from a hundred and eighty odd feet above the sea, they'll never see it!"

"Granted. But it will give me something to do—a man would go mad waiting. Roll up your things and come up with me. There's no need to go fishing to-day."

He picked up the spear. "They won't be here until evening if they come here at all. I'm not going without fish just because you see a sail. There'll be plenty of time after dinner."

He slouched away towards the mangroves while I hurried back to climb the Peak. Charlie was right about there being plenty of time. But I just couldn't go fishing today.

The sails were still in sight, like white handkerchiefs on edge upon a sparkling sea calm as a pond. It was a pleasant labour, carrying stones to build that already highly built cairn. I toiled until midday with many a glance towards the sails. To the south-west, big Lizard Island was very plain. North-west, a distinct pencil outline of ranges indicated the mainland.

I set the flagpole up, placing its butt solidly down between the rocks. As the blanket unfurled a great weight dragged the pole from my hands. In surprise I looked to sea. Throughout some hours of sweating labour I had felt no breath of wind; but now from out towards the Great Barrier rollers were coming in over a nearly flat sea. As I stared, a strong breeze came bowing the grass to the hill side; the mangrove tops sighed tremulously in the forest below. Those three sails were billowing considerably closer. In delight I battled with the long pole. It took twenty minutes of struggle to get the big flag firmly planted in the teeth of a tearing wind. The blanket stood out taut, a square black patch high above the Peak. There was no doubt about the sails now; they were tacking straight for the narrow channel and Coquet.

"They'll anchor this evening at Coquet for a certainty," I laughed. "Oh, if they only will!"

As the tide came in Charlie appeared away below at his camp, lighting up his fire to cook his fish. He stared up at the flag. I waved, but was too excited to go down and eat. Late in the afternoon breakers were smashing on the reef and the sea-line was whipped into a crescent of lathering foam. My heart was sick. If this wind kept up they might not dare attempt to land a dinghy. To banish such thoughts I hurried down the Peak to Charlie.

"They're coming, Charlie! Coming for a certainty; the three vessels will soon make the channel. They must see me as well as the signal; they cannot miss us this time! Pack up your things and be ready when they send a dinghy ashore."

"I'm not going to leave the island."

The words took my breath away. But he meant them.

"Don't be a fool, man. There may not be another chance to get away from this wretched place for months and months. And it's blowing up rough—we'll have to be ready when they send a dinghy ashore. Come on!"

"You are wasting your time," he replied stubbornly. "I won't leave. And what the blazes do you think is going to happen to the wolfram?"

"What wolfram?"

"Why, the tin and wolfram we've got stacked here—nearly a ton of it. Do you think I'm going to leave a hundred pounds behind?"

"Good heavens, Charlie, it's impossible for them to take off that wolfram. Listen to the breakers on the reef! I'm nearly howling like a school kid at the very thought that it may be too rough for them even to send a dinghy ashore for *us*. Never mind the wretched wolfram. I don't want it; all I want is to see Cooktown again. It has cost us far more than a miserable hundred pounds to get it; more than six long months in this wretched place. And if we stayed here just because of the wolfram it would cost us another six months before we could get it transported to Cooktown. If you want the wretched stuff you can easily arrange for one of the Cooktown luggers to pick it up first calm weather she's passing this way. But you'll have to get to Cooktown to do it."

"I'm not going I tell you. Can't you understand that I'm quite satisfied to live here? Go yourself while you have the chance."

"I'm going, Charlie. You'll be all alone. It will be awful here alone."

"Why the blazes should it be awful alone? I've lived alone for years and never noticed. Anyway, now that you've decided to go, what are you going to do with your papers?"

"What papers?"

"Your mining lease. Your' half share in the island."

"You mean our mining rights to the island?" "Yes."

"I'm going to do nothing with them of course. The island is not of the faintest interest to me. I don't care a tinker's cuss what becomes of it — and its mining rights. All I want is to get away from the place."

"Will you transfer your half right to me then?"

And now I realized Charlie was quite in his right mind. He wanted the island not only by right of possession, but officially. I sat down beside him.

"The papers are in your own camp, Charlie, so far as I know. I have never given them a moment's thought. If you haven't got them I don't know where they are."

"Your papers are with mine."

"What do you want me to do then? Transfer my half right to you?"

"Yes. But only if you don't want it." "Give me the papers."

He walked into his camp and came back with the papers, all neatly tied up. They were only the usual blue forms of the mining rights, but perfectly binding legally. From somewhere he produced ink and pen. Quickly I transferred my half share to him and handed him the signed transfer.

"Satisfied?"

"Thanks. The island is no good to you, but I want it. This gives me sole possession. It would be good of you, though, if you could find time in Cooktown to stroll into the warden's office and notify them there."

"Certainly I will. That will be no trouble."

"Thanks."

Carefully he rolled and tied up the papers as I stood up to hurry back to the Peak.

"Well, Charlie, I'm going to stand up on that Peak until it's time to run down to the reef and into the dinghy. I'm positive they'll send a dinghy ashore; I'm leaving the island for good. If you've absolutely made up your mind . . . So long!"

"So long!" he said, and stood up and held out his hand.

We shook hands as I said:

"I'll tell them that you're remaining on the island and that you want stores, when I get to Cooktown. And that you want the wolfram shipped back. Perhaps the ketch may be in port. If so she could land you stores on her next trip. Anyway, the store-keeper will arrange with the skipper when he does arrive."

"All right, if you like. But I don't care. Tell the ketch to call if you see the skipper. By that time I'll know exactly what I'm going to do. Most likely I'll send the wolfram to Cooktown with him and he can bring me back supplies and things I want on his next trip north. I'll write the store-keeper care of the skipper to give you your share."

"Keep it, Charlie. I'm taking not the faintest interest in the stuff. I don't want even to hear of it again. Good-bye."

"Good-bye."

I hurried back to the Peak, and was almost knocked flat by the wind. The mass of tumbling waters filled me with dismay. The two leading cutters were at the mouth of the channel, pitching and rolling like matches in a cauldron.

Towards sundown the nearest lugger was cleaving up the passage between the two islands. Energetically I waved the remnant of my trousers. The lugger driving along with wild speed drew level with the Peak, to tack away suddenly and like a wind-blown sea-gull race for anchorage in shelter of Coquet Island.

I nearly cried. A puff of white smoke suddenly leapt from the stern of the lugger. The wind drowned all sound but—they had fired a shot!

I pranced on the Peak—they had seen me. But by morning no dinghy would be able to live in this rising sea; this might develop into stormy weather that would keep up for weeks. In uncontrollable agitation I ran backwards and forwards along the tip of the Peak, waving those trousers. Scudding clouds raced low to the rising sea, the second lugger came with her decks awash, drew level with the Peak, then she too slewed away, swiftly slipping over beside her mate at Coquet Island. With sickening heart I peered through the gathering gloom at the third lugger only now entering the channel mouth. It would soon be too dark, even if they were game, to launch a boat. The wind was whistling, chilly too.

Ceaselessly waving the signal, I stared down through the spume at the swiftly approaching lugger; she seemed flying as she approached within one hundred yards of the reef and sped along beside it. Frantically I yelled and watched the waves breaking against her bow to scour her decks and fall away in foam at her stern. She rose to a great wave and I saw a cluster of little figures clinging about her bows and a crouching someone up in the rigging. They were gazing up! I snatched at the bamboo pole, tore away the blanket, threw my few things into it, snatched the spear and raced downhill to the reef.

The lugger was already level, I jumped straight at the foam-splashed reef and with waving arms tried to fight my way out as a dinghy like a toy cork was dropped from the stern. The lugger raced into the quickening darkness, the dinghy disappeared. She reappeared, tossing like a fly in a butter churn. Suddenly I realized how high the waves really were. Just out past the reef they were black- green, rolling in to bulge up as they hit the shallow water now on the reef and come sweeping straight in to the mangroves.

Struck on the chest, I was rolled back over the coral but leapt up and yelling plunged out again. It was dark, wind and spume and flying coral sand were blinding and filled my yelling mouth as I struggled to gain deeper water and keep a foothold there. Shadowy arms suddenly jerked me into a dinghy that was tossing in a mad effort to break free of all control.

24

Thank Heaven

A Japanese clad only in a lava-lava with a white sarong around his head gripped the rudder. I gasped up at his inquiring face and shouted:

"Will you take me to Cooktown? I have no money."

"No matter. Any more mens?"

"Yes. There is another man on the island but he will not come away."

The Japanese nodded to the dinghy crew and then commenced a struggle to force the tiny craft back through the rollers breaking on the reef. One Japanese and two strong aboriginals laboured at the oars, another Japanese crouched shouting directions from the bow. The strain told in the knotted throats of the oarsmen as with gritted teeth they pulled the dinghy back foot by foot towards the edge of the reef, the great reef that bound the island in mighty ramparts and whose every mood I knew so well. It seemed fiendishly determined now to hold us to the island. The suspense was pretty awful, staring at the crouching bow man wondering whether he could unerringly signal the rowers the exact moment to strain out over the edge of the reef. He did it, picked the right waves and the dinghy battled through. We had hardly slipped through when the following waves came rolling to crash upon the reef. Highly trained seamanship, a job like that.

It was pitch dark when we plunged over the reef and among the now huge rollers of the deeper water. Each time the dinghy rose to a wave top we saw a dancing masthead light as the lugger sailed in short tacks back and along the channel. She was experiencing a difficult task in picking us up. An hour's hard manoeuvring brought the bouncing dinghy right alongside the lugger. As she rose on the crest of a wave brown hands reached down and I was suddenly sprawled on the deck with the dinghy, my arms around a turtle that was roped helplessly to the deck. As the lugger reeled away into the trough of the sea I scrambled up with singing heart. Good-bye to the island at last! . . . What splendid seamen.

Soon afterwards, to hoarse-voiced commands, the sails came tumbling down, the anchor splashed down to the rattle of the chain. In calmer water we lay beside the lugger's mates under the shelter of little Coquet. Cheery talk broke out as all was made snug for the night; a fire was quickly lighted in the galley, cooking pots were soon bubbling. A hurricane lamp was lashed to the base of the mainmast and it swayed there, a wee faint light. The masthead lights of the other luggers blinked like misty stars.

The blackboy crew rolled on the slippery deck in uncontrollable laughter, the whites of their eyes and teeth gleaming in the swaying lamplight. Apparently my general nakedness and rags caused the merriment; but it really was the fish spear, lying against a coil of rope. Laughingly I threw the spear overboard. And immediately regretted it: that crude weapon had been a friend indeed.

The Japanese captain smilingly produced a clean plate, knife and fork and pannikin.

"You hungry?"

"I've eaten only fish and crabs and latterly potatoes for months."

He nodded, then opened a tin of meat while a grinning blackboy came along with a steaming billy of tea. The smell of it brought back civilization and a ravenous hunger.

"Sugar belonga him?"

I nodded, and he tipped in a big spoonful.

The captain poured a thick helping of condensed milk into the billy can and placed beside it a well-browned sea damper. Meat and tea and sugar, rice and damper and jam!

Trying to laugh away the effort to wait, I thanked him.

"This is heaven!"

"I understand not quite," replied the captain amiably. "Very hungry though you are, sure I am. Sit down and plenty eat of much. There is more will come."

We ate immediately, and my word men *can* eat after a hard day's work at sea.

That was a grand dinner. The crew's meal took a little longer to cook, and by the time it was ready they laughingly put the billy on again for me. I eased over so as to sprawl more comfortably on the deck, then by the dancing rays of the hurricane lamp took stock of my shipmates. Six Japanese sat round a dish of curried fish and rice, while in the bows eight aboriginal seamen ate boisterously—all clothed in the simple lava-lava of the Barrier Seas. The big helpless turtle, its head moving to right and left, its little bright eyes queerly hopeless; two bobbing masthead lights nearby; the black shadow of Coquet Island right against us. And high up over the mast little Coquet blinking brightly. She had always seemed so elusive and far away. Now she was brilliant and flashed more decisively. How the mind of Man has developed when he can set upon the sea a light that, all unattended for six or twelve months at a time, flashes out when sunset comes and goes to sleep at sunrise! The wind was now whining through the halyards, but even that cold wind could not blow away the smell of the lugger with its queer tang of eastern foods. Back in the darkness was a growing thunder as seas rolled pounding on the reef. Away from that island, thank heaven, at last.

The captain stepped down below, then re-appeared on deck with a tin of tobacco, matches, and cigarette papers.

"You smoke?" he smiled, and left me to it.

It was one of those milestones in life that are so long remembered.

Soon afterwards we all turned in. I would rather have sprawled in the old blanket upon the rolling deck and just smoked up at the clouded stars..

But the captain quietly insisted on my taking a bunk below. Into the tiny cabin, dimly lit by a swinging lamp, crawled four of us.

The Japanese were asleep in minutes. It was suffocatingly hot down there in that little walled-in den. Sweat appeared in beads upon the brown naked forms, all coiled up. Their jet-black hair gleamed oilily. By and by big cockroaches came out and scuttled over their moist bodies. The howl of wind came gustily down the companion-way, a muffled roar from away back towards the reef. I wondered how Charlie was doing. Impossible *to* pick him up now even if he changed his mind, which was extremely unlikely. The reef would be an inferno of crashing waters long before morning.

A full hour before the first faint sun ray the lugger was in a bustle. Murmur of tramping feet, an occasional hoarse order, creak of the windlass, grinding of the chain, then rattle of blocks as thankfully I climbed on deck to meet the full force of a howling wind. Pitch darkness, out of which a bright light flashed above. Coquet, too, was on duty, flashing her warning to all. Up rolled the misty sails and, as a Japanese sprang to the tiller, the cutter fell away. A fierce wind roared into the sails, she heeled over, then sped straight into the darkness.

Again that bright, warm light quivered above us. I smiled farewell to Coquet, little friend of many lonely nights.

Splendid seamen, the Japanese. The waves were mountains high, the hour so dark that not even the blackness of the island was visible. An hour later a broad, wavering beam of light shot straight up from out the darkness. Slowly and reluctantly the eastern sky shivered into pink. Almost instantly a half disk of molten gold brightly quivering appeared over the lugger's bows.

Darkness lifted from silvered waters violently tossing. Quickly, the half disk rose to the full and hung clear of the sea. Its dancing rays kissed gold into the foam of waves that came rising to the lugger's bows.

The sun was up. The blackboys marked approval by laughing jokes and a tribal sea song as one of them lit the galley fire. Astern was the Peak of Howick Island rising sheer from the sea. How different the island looked now! With the sun turning gold the grassy Peak it appeared almost romantic. Gladly I watched it growing smaller and smaller.

After breakfast the crew squatted lazily gossiping on deck while ever ready to leap to the captain's sharp orders for the constantly recurring tacking. We anchored by an island again that night, and next day saw us tacking down the long coastline.

"Any peoples live there?" And the captain casually waved an arm towards the dim ranges of our big, empty Peninsula.

"Oh yes. Some big towns in there. Plenty people. Plenty more coming soon. Farming men from England."

"This Peninsula very big country. Only very few your countrymen live north of Cooktown. Why?"

"There are a good many there now. We are pushing out. Many men are now taking up farms. Thousands more are now coming out from England."

"First time I hear these mens in plenty," said the captain thoughtfully. "How long these Englishmens come?"

"Their first boat should be in Brisbane now. Many steamers are following. We shall soon fill up Cape York Peninsula with Australians and Englishmen."

The captain finished his cigarette in silence as we gazed at the big empty Peninsula. It held barely two hundred cattlemen, sandalwood getters, and prospectors. Yet gold and minerals and iron were there; a well-watered country with excellent cattle land.

They killed the poor old turtle. I felt sorry for my miserable fellow voyager, but he provided tasty soup and juicy steaks for every man aboard. During the trip I was treated as an honoured guest; the best of everything was put before me.

The following day we tacked close to two luggers sailing north.

"Could you lay to close beside one and hail her?" I asked the skipper. "I'd like to tell them about my mate. They might be able to land him food should the wind die down."

"Easy that do!" replied the captain confidently, and with perfect manoeuvring he presently brought the lugger within easy hailing distance of the first vessel. She was a Burns Philp pearler, the Japanese aboard as usual spoke good English. I shouted to their captain Charlie's predicament, and asked him to land flour and meat and tea and tobacco and any other suitable items he could spare. He shouted back a promise to do so if possible, and the vessels fell away.

A week later he kept his promise, even to landing a tent.

On the fifth morning, after a glorious sunrise, the white signal station stood out upon Grassy Hill. We came to anchor in the mouth of the Endeavour River within a hundred yards of where Captain Cook beached his vessel so many years ago.

The Japanese doffed their lava-lavas and donned silk shirts and European clothes, taking pains with their personal appearance. Smart men. I thanked them and their captain for the rescue and courtesy; then a black-boy rowed me ashore. I went straight across the street into George Walmsley's shop. Some of the boys were there as usual. They stared in amazement.

"My heavens, it's Jack!" exclaimed George. "The wild man of Borneo! Where have *you* come from?"

Quickly I explained. They laughed hilariously when I gazed into a looking-glass.

"We thought you and Charlie must have taken to the mainland in a nigger's canoe months ago," said George. "The skipper passed your way but saw no signal like you'd arranged."

"*1* signalled all right—did nothing else for hours every day. Charlie may have arranged for some other signal, I don't know. Here, put me into your barber's chair quick and lively, then I'll use your bathroom while you're choosing me a suit of ready-mades. I want to feel civilized."

That afternoon I had an interview with the sergeant of police and explained about Charlie and his lack of supplies, his ill-health, and particularly about his leaving his 'scope and chemicals behind. This led to the police sailing a cutter to the island. By then the lugger had landed stores for Charlie. He refused to leave, but got the police vessel to bring his wolfram back with an order for more stores. Eventually he did leave the island, returned to Cook- town, and later went back up the Peninsula again, looking for gold.

After leaving the police station I strolled around to the warden's office and there officially signed over my share of the island to Charlie, glad to have the matter finally settled.

Then, feeling wonderfully fit and ready to start life all over again, I walked eagerly through the town in search of my old mate Dick.

www.ingramcontent.com/pod-product-compliance
Lightning Source LLC
Chambersburg PA
CBHW031204260626
47169CB00004B/1234